Tell

You

Later

—

W.M. Gonzales

By: W.M. Gonzales

TABLE OF CONTENTS

Chapter 1

It is another hot Tucson day as Isabella stared out the window of her Government class overlooking the football field where graduation would be taking place. In the next two weeks high school would be over and real life would begin she thought to her self. It has been a year since her parents decided that they were no longer happy in Rochester, New York and picked up the family and moved across the country to Tucson, Arizona. Isabella was still bitter about the fact that at the end of her junior year in high school is when they decided that it was no longer bearable to live in the place that she had grown up in for the last 18 years.

Tucson was a hot, dirt filled town. Not like the cool green climate that Isabella was used to. She suddenly found herself surrounded by people who spoke Spanish more frequently than English. The town was primarily Hispanic in nature and was a definite culture shock from the melting pot of Polish, Italian, English and Canadian influences that she grew up with. It had been hard to make friends in her new school where many people had grown up together and they were not interested in the new girl from New York. To fill the gaps of time that was no longer used hanging out with friends, playing soccer or activities on student council, Isabella started taking online travel school classes in hopes of getting a good summer job to help pay for college. Her grades were good but she certainly was not expecting a big scholarship. Her dad was a mechanic and her mom was a secretary. Neither one had a college education and neither one felt it was all that important. Her dad would always tell her that going to school for a skill was much more useful than a piece of paper that says your smart and leaves you with no job and no future. Isabella wasn't sure that she bought into all of that but felt that gaining a skill through travel school would indeed lead to a worthwhile job in the mean time.

The bell rang jolting Isabella out of her daydream. She grabbed her backpack and headed for the door. As she crossed the courtyard her friend Tammy caught up with her. "Hey Isabella. Have you picked up your cap and gown from the book store yet?"

"No, I was just heading that way before I head home. Did you get yours?"

"No, I was going over there too. I can't wait to be done with this place. Two more weeks and we are off to make our mark on the world."

Isabella smiled and nodded. "Yep, off to make our mark."

Tammy was a transplant from Maine. She is a tall girl with long dark hair. She is one of the friendliest, and fun loving people that I have ever met. We became fast friends after having a Trig class together. She had only been here for a year when I moved here. We found that we had a lot of things in common including the interest in traveling after high school. We decided to do the online travel classes together and couldn't wait for summer to do an internship at the airport.

"When do you think we will get our summer assignments at the airport?" She asked with excitement.

"I have no idea. I hope soon." I answered her.

"I am hoping that we get the same airline. It would be a lot more fun."

"I know, me too. I just hope we get jobs out of all of this."

"A job that leads to a super hot pilot would work for me." She says with a giggle.

My face is instantly red at Tammy's comment. I never seem to have the same libido for boys that everyone else has. I am always so busy planning my way out of here and carefully calculating my career plans that I just don't give it much thought. I only seem to attract rockers anyway, and I am not at all attracted to those longhaired metal heads. I much more prefer the preppy or jock crowd but they never seem to give me a second glance. My mom

is always telling me that I am intimidating to boys and that

is why I never get asked out. I think she is just being nice to

her less than glamorous daughter. In my eyes I am an

average girl. With my long curly brunette hair, freckles

and light green eyes I hardly compare to the beauty of the

Hispanic culture that I am surrounded by. "Absolutely, hot

pilots are a must." I joked back with her half-heartedly. We

finished gathering the necessary graduation items and left

campus for home.

When I get home my mom was in the kitchen

preparing for dinner. She turns and smiles. "How was your

day?"

"It was fine. I picked up my cap on gown today."

"Oh let me see it!" My mom says with such

enthusiasm. I think she is more excited about me

graduating then I am.

"Mom, it's a cap a gown. Do I really need to try it

on?"

"Yes you do need to try it on. I need to see how

long it is so I know how long of a dress to buy you for

graduation."

"Mom, anything that comes to the knee is fine.

Trust me."

She looks at me with narrowed eyes as I put the

gown on, and then agrees that she should be able to find me

something that will be hidden by the gown. "Oh, it looks
like you have a letter from Arizona Airlines. I left it on the
dining room table."

I hold my breath with anticipation as I walk into the
dining room to locate the letter. Sure enough it is my
internship assignment. I have been selected to train at the
ticket counter and gate areas with Arizona Airlines for 8
weeks. I look up from the letter with a smile and see my
mom standing at the entry of the dining room watching me
read the letter. "I got selected for Arizona Airlines here in
Tucson. It's an 8 week training internship."

"Congratulations honey." She said as she gave me a hug. "I know how hard you have been working towards this. I am really proud of you."

"Thanks mom. I am going to go call Tammy to see if her assignment came in too. I am hoping that we are together."

"Okay, good luck."

I went to my room, shut the door and dumped my backpack in the middle of the floor. I fell back on my bed and pulled out my cell phone. I am not sure why I didn't just dial her number. I think I was afraid that she would hear the apprehension in my voice. I sent a text message in stead.

Did u get your assignment? I.

Just getting home, stand by.

I sit and start daydreaming about what it will be like to be at the ticket counter in front of the public. I just need to remember that this is a means to see the world while in college. My goal is to do something in medicine. I am not sure what yet but I will start with the prerequisites and go from there. I am torn from my daydream by the vibration of my phone. It is a text from Tammy that read, "*Union Air.*" I then decide to call her.

"Hey girl."

"Hey, Union Air huh?"

"Yeah, but it is only like two counters down from Arizona Air. We will still be together for the most part. I am so excited. Where should we go first?"

"Well, I think first we need to get hired before we can go anywhere." I tell her with a giggle.

"Oh, we will get hired. I mean seriously, who wouldn't see our talent, right?"

We both laugh knowing that our actual work experience doesn't extend much past fast food restaurants.

"Well, two more weeks and we are in the real world sister. It can't come soon enough."

"I know. I just can't wait!" Tammy was bubbling with excitement.

The next two weeks flew by. Senior activities and

finals consumed every minute of every day. Graduation

was the usual ceremonial fanfare. Mom cried, I got a small

scholarship to the community college in Tucson, and we

went for a nice dinner following commencement. All in all

it was a load off of my mind to have it over and behind me.

I was so anxious to start my real life. It was time to make

my own decisions and see some of the world around me.

My mom was always worried that I was trying to grow up

too fast and I think even more worried that I never had any

serious boyfriends. I always felt like she thought that I

should just find some nice boy to marry so he could take

care of me and I wouldn't have to worry about making my

own way. That has never appealed to me, but to her a

marriage at 19 years old and a baby by 20 years old was

good enough for her so why not me?

Chapter 2

The following Monday was the start of my
internship with Arizona Airlines. I had to purchase two
uniforms in order to work at the ticket counter. Everyone
had to adhere to the uniform policy even if it was only a
temporary position. Thankfully my parents helped me with
this since they were pricey and I was hoping to not spend
my graduation money already. I showed up early just in
case I hit traffic or had trouble parking. Tammy and I didn't
report at the same time so we didn't car pool but decided to

try to meet up for lunch if we could. I approached the

counter in uniform and introduced myself surprisingly very

nervous.

"Can I help you?" A short stout lady asked me from

behind the counter with a New York accent.

"Hi, yes, I am Isabella Weston. I am the new

intern."

"Oh, hi. My name is Ruby. Let me show you back

to the manager, Marcia. Have you met her?"

"No, not yet. Thank you."

She motioned for me to follow her and opened the

door behind the ticket counter with her badge. I had been

issued an airport authority badge as a temporary but I had

no idea if I had access to this area on my own. I followed her to a spacious room behind the counter that had a couple of people with headphones on talking into microphones. It sounded like they were talking to the crew on one of the planes but I wasn't sure what their job was. There were other people lurking back there too pulling weather reports for future flights that day and it sounded like weight and balance of the aircraft from what I had learned at school. It was like a secret world back here. We continued to walk through and out the back door of the room. There were offices down a short hallway and one of them led to the manager's office. Her name was Marcia Bradley. She looked very young to be a manager of a major airline. She stood up when we entered the office and immediately came around from her desk to shake my hand with a warm smile.

"You must be Isabella. Hello, my name is Marcia. I am the manager of the Tucson station for Arizona Airlines. It is nice to meet you."

"Hello, it is nice to meet you too."

"Well I see you were able to acquire a uniform. Thank you for coming prepared to start working. Please have a seat and lets talk before we get started." She moved back around her desk and took a seat. I also sat down in the chair in front of her desk. "I see that you just graduated last week from Tucson High School?" She said has she looked at my resume.

"Yes ma'am I did."

"And you successfully finished online travel school with Northwestern Pacific?"

"That is correct."

"What do you hope to learn from us in the next eight weeks Isabella?"

The question threw me a little bit because I actually only wanted to use this job as a means of cheap travel and a way to get me through college. "I am hoping to gain the knowledge and skill to become successful in the travel industry, specifically with Arizona Airlines."

She looked at me for just a moment and sat back in her chair before speaking again. "I too was only 18 years old when I started with this airline. I have been very successful here and believe that with hard work and a passion for the industry, you too could become an integral part of this company."

"I am a hard worker and I am hoping that I can prove that over the next 8 weeks and become a permanent part of the company."

Marcia nodded and kept staring at me. Then she finally spoke and said, "Ok, let's get started. I am going to start you at the gate with Frank today. Here is a book of code entries that you may find useful for ticketing. They are specific to our airline. Oh, and here are some earplugs. You will need these when you meet the flights."

She handed me the small pocket size blue book and the earplugs that look like they are attached to a headband. I put them around my neck and followed her out of the office. While I followed her out of the office and down a back hallway leading to God knows where, I wondered if Tammy was feeling the same nervous energy that I was. I wonder where she is starting today? We finally exited through a side door that led us right to security. Marcia sighed at the length of the line. "You know before nine eleven we would just take the back stairs to the outside and back up the jet way stairs to the gate, but now we all have to go through security every time we want to go down there."

I nodded and smiled, not sure how to respond to that

information. Obviously this situation was annoying to her.

After what felt like an hour but was only about 5 minutes

we were through security and on our way to gate number 4.

Marcia approached the gate desk where a tall thin man was

standing. He smiled and said hello as soon as we

approached. There was no doubt that this was a very gay

man.

"Frank this is Isabella. She is doing an 8-week

internship with us. Today is her first day and I would like

her to work with you here at the gate for today."

He immediately extended his hand to me. "It's nice to meet you Isabella. Come on back here and let's get this party started."

Marcia frowned just slightly but then covered it just as fast. "I will be back later to see how you are doing Isabella. Frank will show you the ropes."

I smiled and said thank you, and she turned and walked away.

"So sweetie, what program did you come out of?"

"Um, Northwestern Pacific Travel School."

He looked at me and nodded. The phone rang behind the counter and he picked it up. "This is Frank. Well, that's just lovely now isn't it? Ok, yeah, we got it."

He hung up and turned to me. "Well, the next flight just canceled out of Seattle so we need to make an announcement and then try to book all of these people on other flights out of here tonight if possible." He took my book from my hand and opened it up and laid it down on the counter. "This is the bulk of what you need to know about reissuing tickets. It's just you and me. Are you ready?"

I didn't have words because I was completely terrified. I just nodded in agreement.

"Before I make this announcement and the lines begin to form, let's make sure that you can log in."

I stepped up to the computer and logged in with the temporary access that I had been granted.

"Ok well, welcome to the club." Frank snickered and picked up the microphone. "Ladies and gentlemen flight 2025 from Seattle has canceled due to a mechanical issue. This means that the continuing service to Chicago will be canceled. Please approach the counter for assistance rescheduling your departure. Thank you."

By the time I turned around the line was as far as the eye could see. Frank rejoined me and said, "Just follow my lead." I nodded and logged into the flight information screen for all of the Tucson departures. After the first dozen passengers I was getting the hang of rescheduling a flight and putting a passenger on another carrier. It amazed me that Frank could concentrate on what he was doing and guide me at the same time. I guess that's why Marcia paired me with him. He really was good.

I wasn't sure how much time elapsed but before I knew it everyone was gone. Frank was closing out the flight and putting up a new message on the screen behind us announcing the cancelation of flight 2025.

"You did good kid. That's quite a way to start your first day."

I smiled and was appreciative for the compliment. "Thank you, I hope that I was some help anyway."

"We have about a 30 minute reprieve and then we need to meet the next flight. I am going to step away for a minute to make a phone call."

I nodded in acknowledgement. Once he stepped away I sent a quick text to Tammy.

How's it going? Just had a canceled flight here, it was totally overwhelming.

It only took a few seconds before a response from her reciprocated.

It is so awesome over here. Going to the APP with crew here after work. Want to go too?

What is the APP? I asked.

It's a bar around the corner. It stands for the Airport Pub.

I don't know if you realize this but we are only 18 years old?

Everyone says we won't get questioned if we are in uniform.

Let's go. What's the worst thing that could happen? We get asked to leave?

Oh brother, seriously? I spent all of these years following the rules, being good, being no trouble to my parents to jeopardize everything on underage drinking, drinking and driving, and a possible arrest? But I typed in, *Let's go together.*

I could almost feel her excitement through the phone. *Yeah! I will meet you in front of the Sky Cap desk in front of Union Air.*

Just then Frank returned. I quickly shoved my phone back in my pocket. "Anything earth shattering happen while I was gone?"

"Nope. It was all quiet."

"The next flight will land at five. Let's go down the jet way and I will show you how to drive it." He quickly turned and started toward the secured door that passengers disappear down or appear from. I scurried behind him before he disappeared down the intimidating hallway. It was hot in there. You would think that they would air condition these in Tucson. It is a hundred degrees out here in the summer making this short walk almost unbearable.

We reached the end of it and I stared at the control panel in front of me. Frank broke through my silent fearful thoughts. "When the plane comes in they will stop the wheels on that white line. Once the blocks go under the wheels you will drive the jet way up to the door of the plane." He showed me how to turn the wheels to go side to side and front and backwards. The plane had landed by then and they were directing it into the gate area. Frank motioned for me to put my earplugs in. Once the plane stopped and the blocks were in place he motioned for me to start my first drive up to the plane. I adjusted the wheels so I could pull up to it strait, then just before I started moving forward Frank leaned over to me and pulled one earplug out of my ear and said, "Go slow because if you hit the side of the plane too hard you could knock it over with this thing."

My eyes were as big as saucers. Are you kidding me? I could knock the plane over? My stomach was immediately in knots and I could tell that Frank was

amused with a slight grin on his face. He dropped the

earplug back into my ear and motioned for me to get going.

I slowly moved the Jetway toward the plane and left a

small gap between the edge of the plane and the Jetway.

Frank walked over and looked and then said, "Come

closer." I slowly complied until I was touching the plane.

He motioned for me to stop. We then secured the area and

the door to the plane opened. The flight attendant smiled

back at us and then people began filing out of the plane.

Once every passenger was off the pilots walked off

of the plane and into the Jetway. One of them looked at

Frank and said, "For a minute I didn't think you were going

to let us off of this plane." He said it with a smirk but I know he was letting me know that it took too long for me to get the Jetway up to the plane.

Frank pointed a thumb at me and said, "Woman driver."

They laughed and kept walking and I could feel my face get very hot and I am sure very red. I followed them silently suddenly looking forward to the illegal drink that I was going to have after work. I could use it.

The rest of the day was much less eventful and I gained more confidence with each flight. Before I knew it the day was over. Frank, Ruby and Kate all told me goodnight and that they would see me in the morning. I started collecting my purse from my locker so I could meet up with Tammy when Tony asked me what I was doing after work. Tony was a college student that had been working with Arizona Air for the last two years. He was reserved, clean-cut, blonde hair and a boyish smile. I liked him as soon as I met him. He was very comfortable to be around and had a very calm, easygoing personality. He was in school for his MBA and wanted to move up in the airline industry.

I immediately felt embarrassed about where I was going after work. I wonder if he was going there too? He knows that I am underage, what will he think of me? Why do I care, I just met him? "I am meeting my friend Tammy and we are going to the APP with some of the Union Air

crew."

He looked at me for a long moment and then said,

"Didn't you just graduate from high school?"

For the second time today my face was hot and

flushed. "Yeah." Was all I could manage to squeak out

through my embarrassment. "Do you want to join us?"

Tony just smiled that sweet boyish smile and said,

"No thank you, I have a hot date with my Marketing

Management book and a pot of coffee."

Still feeling embarrassed and guilty I answered,

"Ok, well if you change your mind." I didn't finish my

sentence because I didn't really know what to say, that I

would be at the bar, or that I would be at the police station

being booked for underage drinking?

He nodded at me slowly. "Have a good night. I will

see you tomorrow."

"You too. See you tomorrow." I smiled sheepishly.

As he walked away I wondered why I was not more

attracted to him. He is everything that I always tell myself

that I want in a man. Yet I feel no real attraction to him

other than a potentially very comfortable friendship. I snap

myself out of my short daydream pondering life and begin

to walk toward my meeting place with Tammy. She was

already there when I arrived and bubbling from her day.

She hooked her arm in mine as we began walking toward

the parking lot.

"Oh my God what a great day. Wait until I

introduce you to my coworkers. They are so cool." She

practically squealed when she was telling me about the

people that she had met today. We made our way to her car

and she was still talking a mile minute when she pulled out

of the parking lot. The APP was literally around the corner

from the airport. It was a total dive bar that I never would

have noticed if someone didn't point it out to me. I

reluctantly got out of the car, and Tammy was already

making her way to the door where her coworkers were all

arriving at the same time. She then turned and motioned for

me to hurry up so we could all enter together. When I

caught up to her she started introducing me to her new

friends.

"Guys this is Isabella. She is interning at Arizona

Air." Everyone smiled and said hi. "Isabella, this is Tim,

Mike, Greg, Debbie, Brenda and Kelly."

"Hi, it's nice to meet you." I said as I shook each

persons hand.

"Let's go in." Mike directed us through the door

and to a back table. The bar was dark and smelled like stale

beer. Country music was playing on the jukebox. Mike

walked right up to the bar while we were all taking our

seats and ordered two pitchers of beer. I was grateful that

he had taken charge of what we were all drinking. I had no idea what I would've ordered on my own. Tim met him up at the bar and got frosted glasses for us while Mike carried the pitchers back to the tables we occupied. They poured and distributed glasses to everyone at the table. I didn't know whether to offer money to him or not, but nobody made a move to offer help with the tab so I took my beer and stayed silent and began listening to the chatter around me.

Mike was definitely the life of the party. He talked loudly with Greg as they started some crude conversation about another girl who worked at another airline. Apparently Greg visited her often and freely gave details about their sexual activities that they participated in

nightly. Tammy was chatting away with the other girls at

the table about the events of today. You would think that

Tammy had known them for years the way she could just

slip into conversation. I wished I wasn't so socially

awkward and weird. I always have a hard time starting

conversation. I slowly sipped my beer and quietly observed

and listened to the people around me.

"How was your first day?" It was Tim who was

talking to me. He was smiling while waiting for me to

devise an answer.

Feeling suddenly a little shy I answered, "It was

fine, busy."

Tim has dark brown eyes, wavy brown hair and is very slender. He smirked back at me. "Fine and busy? Did you like it? Was everyone nice to you?"

"Oh yes. It was a lot of fun and everyone was very nice to me."

"Where did they put you today?"

"Gate."

"You were at the gate on your first day? Wow, that's tough. Who were you working with?"

"I was working with Frank."

"Aw yes, Frank. He didn't beat you up too badly?"

"No, he was nice to me. He scared the crap out of me when he told me that I might push the plane over with the Jetway if I wasn't careful though."

Tim let out a booming laugh. "Is that what he said? That is a little overstated. I am sure if you really hit it full steam ahead you might be able to do that, but otherwise I think you're safe." He continued to laugh and I almost felt silly for saying anything. What a fool to be so gullible.

Tim leaned over and refilled my glass. I hadn't realized that I had almost finished the entire drink. I could already feel its effects even after just one. "Who else besides Frank did you meet today?"

"Um, well I met Ruby, Kate, Tony, and of course my manager Marcia."

Tim nodded as if in thought. "Tammy says that you are both starting college in the fall. Are you going to U of A or Pima?"

"I have a scholarship to Pima so I will get my prerequisites out of the way there first."

"What are you going to study?"

"I am leaning toward Radiography."

"So what's your interest in the airlines if medical is your field of choice?

That was a loaded question. I didn't want anyone to know that I only intended for this to be temporary to get me through school and give me the opportunity to travel. I

would never get hired permanently if that got out.

"I love travel and if I go in flight the medical

background will benefit me."

He seemed to be satisfied with my lame answer and

I hoped it would tame any further questioning.

"Are you in college too?"

That seemed to be a very amusing question for him

because it drew the attention of Mike and Greg as well. He

laughed and said, "No. No, I am not in college."

Mike and Greg both laughed as well. I felt

uncomfortable at the humor they all found in this question

and started to turn my attention back to the girls. They were talking about a party that Debbie was having on Saturday. It was a birthday party for her husband, Charles. He was a pilot and would be home this Saturday for his birthday. She was planning a surprise party and had invited everyone at the table. Tammy had already accepted the invitation for the both of us.

Before my drink could get filled for the third time I announced that we needed to get going. Tammy pouted but took my queue. As we started to get up to go, Tim handed me a napkin with his cell number on it. Under his number it said, "In case you need anything."

I read it and looked back up at him. "Thank you. I appreciate it."

We then made our way to the door and left. Tammy

was talking a mile a minute. "They are all so cool. They

were right nobody questioned us at all in uniform. The

party on Saturday is going to be awesome. I hear that

Debbie lives in the Foothills in an amazing house."

I nodded in agreement as we left trying to decipher

if she was okay to drive. I hadn't paid any attention to how

much she had to drink. "Are you okay to drive? How much

did you drink?"

"I am fine. I only had one."

Great, now I am the lush in this scenario.

"Did Tim give you his number when we were

leaving?"

I nodded in affirmation and showed her the napkin as she started the car.

"In case you need anything, huh? He likes you."

"Oh he does not. He is just being polite."

"Keep telling yourself that but he likes you. He is like 25 or something. Just think what you could learn from him." She winks which makes me blush yet again today. I hit her arm and tell her to shut up and drive.

Chapter 3

The rest of the week flew by. I was getting more and more comfortable with each task that I was learning and was working independently most of the time. Everyone that I worked with was pleasant but I felt most comfortable around Tony. He had such a calming effect on me and was easy to talk to and be around. We ate lunch together every day and I found myself talking to him like we had been friends for years.

"Are you going to Debbie's party on Saturday?" I asked him when we were at lunch on Friday.

Tony looked at me puzzled and asked, "Debbie who?"

"I guess that means no." I laughed. "She works at Union Air and is married to some pilot. She is short with dark hair, very pretty. It is her husbands birthday and she is having a surprise party."

He shook his head slightly while listening to me. "I know who your talking about and no I am not going to the party."

I looked at him puzzled. Was I detecting dislike for Debbie in his voice or am I just reading into this? "No because you weren't invited or no because you don't like her?" I cringed after asking the question not liking how that came out.

"Isabella, I don't hang out with that group of people. We don't have the same interests."

"What are your interests?"

"I like to work on restoring my truck, I study a lot, go to movies, read, things like that."

"And they don't have these interests?"

He paused before answering. "No, I don't believe they do."

"What do you believe their interests are?" I am prying now and there is no doubt about it. I wanted to know why he didn't like them.

"I don't know Isabella I just don't think their interests are same as mine."

He almost sounded annoyed now and I decided to drop the subject. I really liked the friend I had made in him and didn't want to make him mad. He obviously doesn't like them for some reason. "What kind of truck are you restoring?"

This was definitely a happier subject because his face brightened immediately.

"It's a 1968 Ford Truck. I just put a 360 FE block engine in and a new 2 ¼" dual exhaust with stock oval mufflers."

I know nothing about cars except for when to put
gas in the tank but I listened attentively and nodded with
enthusiasm. "I would love to see it when it's done. It
sounds great."

"It won't be much longer just some rear end work
and then paint and seats. I will let you know when it's done
and we can take it cruising."

I know that Tony is not the cruising type and
laughed along with him. "Cruising. I will hold you to that."

We both laughed knowing that neither one of us
would ordinarily do this for fun but would take it for a spin
down Speedway just to celebrate its resurrection. Lunch
was over and we walked back to the ticket counter together

making small talk. We passed the Union Airline counter and I saw Tammy there with the same group that all met up earlier in the week. I smiled and gave a discreet wave as we passed. Tony didn't even give them a glance.

The day came to a close and I met up with Tammy on the way out. "I can't wait for the party tomorrow!" She was giddy just thinking about it. "We can ride together if you want. Do you want to crash at my house after so you don't have to drive all of the way home late at night?"

I shrugged since I hadn't really thought about it. "Yeah, that sounds good. What time do you want to meet up?"

"We need to be there by 8:30 since it is a surprise party and all."

"Okay, I will meet you at your house by 8:00."

"Hey, I saw you walking with Tony today. What's the scoop with him? Has he asked you out?"

"No, it's not like that. We are friends. I like him and we have a lot in common."

She raised a brow to me as if to say what is the problem then. "Is he coming to the party too?"

"I asked him but he said no. He has a lot to do." I didn't want to let on to Tammy that I didn't think he liked them over there. I am not sure why I felt like I needed to hide it, but I didn't want to start any issues when I wasn't even sure there was an issue. She seemed to be satisfied

with this answer and dropped the subject. "I will call you

tomorrow before I head over to your house." I quickly

stated before the conversation could expand further.

"Okay, talk at you tomorrow." She said as we

parted ways toward our own vehicles.

Chapter 4

Saturday was like most for me. I cleaned my room,

did my laundry and started looking at my college

registration information. I needed to register in two weeks.

The Radiography program was intense and moved fast.

They basically dictated to you what classes you were taking

and in what order. This way they had complete classes

going through clinicals at the same time. I couldn't wait.

Now that I had decided on my major this had become my

passion and I was anxious to get started. The day passed

and I got ready to go to Tammy's house. My parents were

out to dinner but I had already let them know that I would

be staying with her tonight. They never questioned or

disapproved since I was never in trouble and have never

given them a reason to worry. I pulled out of my driveway

and called her on my cell phone while I was driving to let

her know I would be there in 20 minutes.

When I got to Tammy's she was ready to go. She was naturally stunning in her Lucky jeans and fitted black t-shirt. Her long dark hair fell on her shoulders in waves. I wish I possessed natural beauty. I had on a denim mini skirt and peasant top and had pulled my hair back into a high ponytail. She was bubbling with excitement at the anticipation of what the night would bring. "I will put your bag in my room and then we will go." She said as she almost ran through the house. The house was quiet and I didn't think anyone was there.

"Where is everyone?"

"My parents went to a movie. Hey, I had my sister pick up a bottle of wine for us to bring as a gift. I didn't know what to give a pilot for his birthday."

"Good thinking. That was nice of her to do that for us."

"It was cool of her, and thank God she already had plans or I am sure that she would have asked to come with us in hopes of landing her own pilot."

We both laughed knowing that Tammy's sister, Sue, was clearly at the U of A to find a man with a future. Building her own future was taking too much time and effort.

We arrived at the party at 8:20. We parked around the corner at Debbie's request so as not to tip off her husband. When we got up to the door I was starting to feel nervous. This was not like most house parties we had gone to in high school. This house was expensive. It was located right in the heart of the Foothills with breathtaking views of the Catalina Mountains. The door opened and Debbie welcomed us in. We set the wine on the gift table and headed over to the bar out side to get drinks. I got a soda and Tammy took a beer. Just as we were turning from the bar Tim had walked up behind me and I almost crashed into him.

"Glad you made it."

My face flushed right away. "Thanks" Was all I could think of to say.

Tammy giggled at how uncomfortable I looked. "Is Mike here yet?"

Tim replied, "He is over by the pool."

Tammy didn't say another word as she turned and went looking for Mike. Obviously this is the reason she was so excited about the party. Mike had playboy looks with jet-black hair and stunning blue eyes. He was always the center of attention much like Tammy. They were two naturally beautiful people. So much for the pilot she was hoping to land, she had just set her sites on Mike.

As she left Tim looked at what drink I was holding in my hand. "A soda? Are you sure you wouldn't rather have a glass of wine or something?"

"I didn't want to make Debbie mad being underage and all."

Tim laughed, "Trust me, she won't be mad. Let me get you a glass of white wine." He walked up to the bartender and brought me back the wine. As he handed it to me he took the soda. Secretly I was grateful for the wine because I was nervous just being here. I had just taken a sip when Debbie announced for everyone to gather in the family room for her husband's arrival. Tim grabbed my hand and led the way. We all stood quietly in the family room waiting for Debbie's husband, Charles, to arrive. I

could feel Tim standing closely behind me. I felt nervous

with him that close to me but didn't move away either. I

could not see Tammy anywhere and wondered where she

was. We then heard the front door open and Charles walked

in. We all shouted surprise and startled the life out of the

poor man. He was definitely surprised by the look on his

face. He looked around for Debbie who came up beside

him and then gave him a hug and a kiss. They were a

dashing couple together. Tim then leaned down close to my

ear and said, "Let's go back outside." He grabbed my hand

and I followed. He led me to the edge of the raised hot tub

and motioned for me to sit next to him. I did as I glanced around for Tammy. Where could she be?

"Tammy tells me that you have a birthday coming up too."

"She did? How did that come up?"

"I was gathering information about you." He winked and laughed.

I laughed as well and answered his question. "Next week I turn 19."

"Are you doing anything to celebrate?"

"No plans right now. My parents usually take me to dinner."

He nodded slightly and said, "I would like to take you to dinner for your birthday as well if you would do me the honor. Are you busy next Friday?"

I did not see that coming. Tim was attractive enough I guess but I didn't feel any great attraction to him. Come to think of it, I never feel any great attraction to anyone as of yet. My mother keeps telling me to get out more and that I am too fussy where boys are concerned. However, this is not a boy, this is a man. I am still not sure just how old he is but he is definitely in his early to mid 20's. "No, I am not busy. I would like to go to dinner on Friday."

"Great, I will pick you up at 7. Where do you live?"

I did not want him picking me up at my house. I would have to introduce him to my parents and this is just a casual birthday dinner not a serious boyfriend. "Why don't I meet you somewhere?"

He looked at me questioningly for a moment. "I will meet you at the APP at 6:30 and we can go from there."

"Sounds good." Tim said with a wary smile.

At that point I saw Brenda and her husband walking toward us. She stopped and said hello and introduced us to her husband, Martin. Brenda is fairly new with Union Air and this was the first social event that she had attended with her husband in tow. Brenda is a petite blond that I am sure was a cheerleader in high school. She couldn't have been more than 23 or 24 years old but had 2 children and was married to a cop. Martin looked like he felt out of place. I immediately set down my wine as if it wasn't mine.

"Hi Tim, hi Isabella. This is my husband, Martin."

"Hi Martin, it's nice to meet you." Tim said as he shook his hand.

"Hi." I said and I shook his hand as well.

Martin muttered a hello but clearly didn't want to be there. Brenda began talking to Tim enthusiastically about their day at work and then explained to Martin that Tim is her trainer and very patient with her. Martin nodded thoughtfully and said nothing. There was an uncomfortable pause as I looked around and saw Kelly and her husband

Tom sitting near the pool. I excused myself and began

walking towards them to say hello. Kelly saw me

immediately and waved a hello. She introduced me to her

husband who is a pilot in the Air force and we all

immediately engaged in conversation.

"Great party, huh?" Kelly commented.

"Yeah. This is a beautiful house."

"Obviously private pilots make more than military

pilots do." Kelly said and laughed. Her husband Tom

chuckled and nodded too. He seemed like a nice guy.

"Base housing isn't quite as fancy as all of this."

Tom offered in case I was confused.

"Hey, have you seen Tammy anywhere? I haven't seen her since we got here a couple of hours ago."

Kelly shook her head. "No. I didn't even know that she was here."

At that moment I saw Tammy and Mike walk from the house out into the back yard where we all were. She was holding his hand and had a disheveled and satisfied look about her. What had she been up to? Certainly she wasn't messing around with Mike in someone else's house? I waved and caught her attention. Mike saw me walking toward them and said something to her and stepped away. She walked toward me and grabbed arm and kept walking with me away from everyone. She whispered as we walked.

"Sorry I left you for so long. How's the party going?"

"Where have you been? I couldn't find you anywhere? And why is your hair all messed up?"

She giggled and reached up to fix her hair as if she knew where to smooth it down. "I had sex with Mike."

"You what? You just met him!"

"Shh. I know, I know. It wasn't my intention. It just happened and it was so amazing. That man knows what he is doing."

I held my hand up to stop her before she gave me any of the gory details. "We should go before you go in for round two."

Tammy laughed, "No, come on, let's stay for a little while longer. Please?"

"Just a little while, Tammy, I am serious."

She shook her head in agreement and squealed happily. "Let's get a drink."

I pulled her arm back before she sprinted away. "Be careful, Brenda's husband is a cop and he is here with her."

Before she could say anything more Mike walked up behind her with a drink for each of them. He handed it to her and slid his hand in the back pocket of her jeans. Tim was right behind him and walked up to me with a fresh glass of white wine. As Tim handed me my glass he leaned over and whispered in my ear, "It looks like Tammy and

Mike are having a good time."

My face was beet red. Did Mike run over there and

tell him or was it that obvious? I shrugged my shoulders as

if I didn't know what he was talking about and glanced at

Tammy who was whispering and giggling with Mike.

"Thank you for the drink. Where's Brenda's

husband?" I looked around as I asked.

"They already left. I don't think Martin was having

fun." Tim laughed as he watched me look around paranoid.

Another hour went by and so did two more glasses

of wine. I was feeling a little tipsy and kept an eagle eye on

Tammy before she disappeared again on me. I finally got

her attention and motioned that we should go. She nodded

ok. I told Tim that I was leaving and he offered to walk me

out to the car since Tammy and Mike had already slipped

out. I was holding my breath hoping that I wasn't going to

walk up on them mauling each other at the car.

As I suspected they were already there embraced in

a steaming kiss and Mike's hands all over her. I stopped

walking so I wouldn't intrude. Tim saw as well and we

stopped a safe distance from the car in hopes that they

would come up for air soon. Not knowing what to do or say

I stood looking at the ground. Tim turned toward me and

lifted my chin up to his. He looked at me for just a moment

and leaned down and kissed me so softly that I wasn't sure

it had really happened. "Good night Isabella. I am looking forward to dinner on Friday."

I smiled back up at him. "I am looking forward to it too."

Tim smiled back at me with such sincerity it warmed my heart. "Come on let's go break that up over there or you'll never get home." He grabbed my hand and started pulling me toward the car. When we got there Tim banged his hand on the trunk as we approached. "Break it up until you can get a room you two."

Mike looked up over Tammy's head and then pulled his hands up. I am sure he had a hand in her pants. I can't believe her right now. What is she thinking? Tammy didn't turn around as she caught her breath. Mike hugged her and

smiled over at us. He leaned down gave her another kiss

and said something in her ear that made her laugh. Then he

broke away from her and looked over at me and said,

"Have a good night Isabella."

"Bye Mike." Tim was still holding my hand and

pulled it up to his mouth and kissed it before letting it go.

"Good night Isabella."

"Good night Tim."

"Good night Tammy." Tim said to her.

"Bye Tim." Tammy said without ever turning

around.

The boys walked away and I approached Tammy.

"Wow." She still didn't look up at me.

"I know how this looks Isabella, but I really like him."

I nodded in agreement. "I can see that."

She peeked up at me and we both started laughing.

"Are you sure about this Tammy? People say he's a player you know. I just don't want you to get hurt."

"I know. I have heard it too, but I just don't know what to say. I feel like I can't keep my hands off of him when I am near him."

"I hadn't noticed that. Are you sure that's how you feel?" I was laughing as I said this to her.

She looked up and slapped my arm. "Shut up. Let's

go home."

We got in the car and headed to her house.

"So how was it?"

I could see her smile even in the dark of the car.

"My God Isabella I didn't know it could be like that. I

came so hard that I was sure the entire party could hear me

scream."

My face was red but she couldn't tell in the car.

"Wow, that sounds intense Tammy. I am happy for you."

"Me too!" She giggled.

I filled her in on the parts of the party that she

missed while she was off having her ultimate orgasm. I left

the part about going to dinner with Tim out for now. I am

not sure why I am so secretive about this date but I just

didn't want to enter into any discussion of us doing what

her and Mike had just done. I just don't see that with him.

When we finally got to her house we were both tired and

went right to bed.

I slept sound until my phone rang at 9 waking me

up.

"Hello?"

"Bella? It's Tony. Did I wake you up?"

Tony and I hadn't been friends for very long but I liked it when he called me Bella. "Yeah, but that's okay I needed to get up and start my day."

"I am sorry. You should just blow me off when you are tired and resting."

I smiled at his kind words. Tony is the nicest most comfortable friend ever. "No, no, don't be silly. What's up anyway?"

"I was just wondering if you wanted to go bowling tonight."

"Bowling?"

"Yeah, you know, you throw the ball and hits pins and they fall down."

"I know what bowling is silly, I just haven't done that in a long time. It sounds like fun. What time?"

"How about 6 at Cactus Bowl. We can have pizza before we play."

"That sounds great. I will see you there." I hung up and saw Tammy staring at me.

"Did I just hear you say that you were going bowling tonight?"

"Yeah, why?"

She just shook her head in disgust. "Nothing, nothing, I am sure that it will be fun."

I through my pillow at her and laughed. "It will be for your information."

"Are you going with Tony?"

"How did you know that?"

"Because he is always trying so hard to get your attention, that's why."

"No he's not. We are just good friends."

"I think you are his good friend. I think he would like more."

"No, you are wrong. You don't know him like I do."

She smiled slightly and dropped the subject. We finally made our way down stairs to have some breakfast when the doorbell rang. Tammy answered it and then came back into the kitchen after a few minutes. Her face glowed

as she held a beautiful bouquet of red roses.

"I take it from the look on your face that those are

from Mike?"

She nodded affirmative and was a little teary eyed.

She was falling quickly for this guy. I seriously hoped he

wouldn't break her heart.

"They are beautiful."

She nodded again trying not to cry. She put them in

water and set them in her room.

"Tammy, I am truly happy for you, but promise me

you will be careful. Okay? Just be careful."

"I will, don't worry, really. I know what I am

doing."

I drove home shortly after breakfast so I could

shower up and start my day. I was looking forward to my

evening with Tony. Although I knew that my evening

wouldn't consist of a tryst in someone else's house, a night

of bowling sounded divine.

Chapter 5

I walked into the bowling ally and looked around hoping that I would see Tony as soon as I walked in. I pulled out my phone to send a text to see if he was here yet. Just as I hit send I felt Tony touch my shoulder. "Hi Bella."

I looked up and smiled. "Hi Tony." I reached over and gave him a hug.

He smiled back like Tony always does making me forget how awkward I am. "Are you ready for some pizza and bowling?"

I shook my head still smiling. We decided to take our pizza and soda to the lane and eat while we bowled. It was so much fun and we laughed endlessly as we went from throwing a strike to a gutter ball. We were all over the place but we didn't care.

"So how was the party last night?"

I shrugged a little bit before answering. "It was okay I guess. A lot of people were there."

"That's good. I am glad that you had fun."

I quickly changed the subject knowing that Tony was just being polite. "Have you been working on your truck?"

"You know it. I am hoping that it will ready to go in a couple of weeks."

"Good, because I am waiting patiently to go cruising. Don't forget."

"Bella, I would never forget."

Before I knew it we had eaten all of the pizza and bowled three games. "We should call it a night since we have to be in to work early tomorrow." I announced half-heartedly.

"I agree, it is getting late. Let me walk you to your car."

We walked out side by side not saying anything. It was just comforting being around him. When we got to my car I unlocked it but Tony reached over and opened the

door for me. Chivalry is not dead, I thought to myself.

"Thank you Tony. I had a great time."

"Me too Bella. Let's do it again soon."

"I would like that." I gave him another hug and then

got into my car. Tony closed the door after me. As I pulled

away I thought about Tony and how successful he was

going to be someday. He is so put together and sure of

himself and such a gentleman.

Chapter 6

The week flew by and before I knew it, it was Friday. My birthday wasn't until tomorrow but dinner with Tim was tonight. Just as I was getting my things to leave, Tony walked up to me and handed me a card. I grinned and took it from his hand. I sheepishly looked up at him. "How did you know?"

"I know lots of things grasshopper."

I laughed and opened the card. It was a singing card that played *She's Got A Way About Her* by Billy Joel. It was a sweet card and made me feel so happy. "Thank you

Tony. I love it." I hugged him and we stood there for a

minute.

"You're welcome and happy birthday. Are you

doing anything to celebrate?"

I immediately felt uncomfortable but didn't want to

lie. "Well, I am going to dinner tonight with Tim and

tomorrow with my parents."

I couldn't read the look on Tony's face and it

bothered me that I couldn't tell what he was thinking. Then

he smiled slightly and said, "Have a good night. I hope you

have fun."

Feeling guilty for some unknown reason I said, "Thank you." I said it so quietly it was even hard for me to hear. I closed my locker and started to walk out.

"Be careful Bella." Tony said softly.

I paused and looked back at him confusion on my face not understanding what I was being careful of. "Okay Tony. I will be." Was it coincidental that I had told Tammy the same thing about Mike?

He smiled and walked away.

I continued out of the department when Kate came up beside me and began walking next to me.

"You know there is nothing wrong with Tony."

I was startled at her statement. "I know that. Why would I think there was anything wrong with Tony?"

"Because you don't really see him."

I stopped and looked at her. I didn't know what she was trying to say to me but I was feeling mad at her. She stopped as well but said nothing more. She looked at me for a moment and then walked away. I watched her leave and continued to stand there speechless. What the hell was that all about? Did Tony say something to her about me? No, I don't think he would do that. If I had upset him he would have told me. I turned and started walking again. I needed to hurry home so I wouldn't be late meeting Tim.

When I got home I slipped on a black sheath dress and some sling back heals. I curled my hair with a big curling iron to have organized silky curls instead of my usual out of control curls. I touched up my makeup and applied some fresh lip-gloss. That should do it. I got in my car and headed for the APP. When I got there, Tim was already waiting for me in the parking lot. He looked handsome in grey slacks and a royal blue dress shirt. He was leaning against his car when I pulled in. I got out and locked my car.

As I got out Tim walked up beside me. "Why don't we take your car and park it at my place. It will be safer there and we can leave for dinner from there."

I felt a little nervous about going to his place but I said ok and got back in the car. I followed him to midtown to a townhouse on Adam's street. I pulled in front and parked on the street. Tim had pulled in the driveway. I got out and walked over to him.

"Let me get the door for you." He went to the passenger side and opened his car door for me. I got in and felt grateful that he hadn't invited me in just yet. We pulled out and headed to the restaurant.

"I hope *Edward's In The Foothills* is okay."

"It sounds great."

"Have you ever been there?'

"No I haven't."

He smiled. "Good, I like showing people new things. You are going to love it. The views of the city are spectacular."

He was right. We sat at a table near the window and looked out at the city lights.

"This is beautiful."

"I am glad that you like it." Tim then ordered a bottle of Cabernet Sauvignon.

After we ordered and the wine had been poured, Tim lifted his glass to toast mine and said, "Happy birthday Isabella and many more."

I smiled and touched my glass to his. "Thank you." I drank the wine that warmed the very core of my body. We were quiet for a few minutes just enjoying the moment.

"Next time I will cook for you. I am not bad you know."

I smiled thankful that he wasn't hoping for my cooking. "I would like that. How long have you lived in your townhouse?"

"Just a few months. I rent the place with Greg."

"Greg? I didn't know that you were that close. I thought you were friends with Mike."

"I am friends with Mike but I room with Greg."

Greg kind of scared me honestly. He was abrupt and talked vulgar about women. I tried to never make eye contact with him ever. The look on my face must have said a thousand words.

"He's harmless. He just talks a good game."

Our entrées came and we ate and made small talk. We talked about New York and what it was like to grow up there. He told me about how he grew up in Las Vegas but moved to Tucson in high school with his mom when his parents divorced. He had 2 brothers and 3 sisters. Only his younger sister was here in Tucson. Everyone else was older and had stayed in Vegas.

"How old are you Tim?"

"Why? Are you nervous that I am too old for you?"

I flushed right away. Was I that obvious? "No, I was just wondering. I mean, you know how old I am."

"I am 24."

Yikes, Tammy was right he is 5 years older than me. That seems like a lifetime when you are just starting college and a career. Oh no, wonder if he expects me to have sex with him? I have only done that once in high school and that was awful. The worst, not at all the steamy, caring, romantic dream that girls read about. That boy literally stuck himself in me, finished his business and then was done and gone. That was stupid on my part. I never should have given into him and it was certainly the last time that I did that. I felt so violated and ashamed of myself. I was trying not to panic at the thought of a repeat performance.

"What are you thinking about Isabella?"

"Nothing, just thinking." I looked a little startled.

He looked thoughtfully at me and we sat and finished the wine and then dessert. When we were done he drove us back to his place where my car was parked. Inside I was panicking and hoping that he wouldn't pick up on it. When we got there he pulled in the driveway and turned off the car. He turned in the seat and looked at me. I looked down at my hands not knowing what to do next.

"Isabella, look at me."

I looked up but didn't say a word.

He took my chin and leaned down and kissed me. This time the kiss was deeper, passionate. His tongue entered my mouth and moved slowly. I relaxed immediately and enjoyed every minute of his tenderness. When he pulled away he said, "Don't be scared of me Isabella. You make me feel incredible." He leaned over and kissed me again but harder this time. He pressed against my lips and his tongue moved against mine with more urgency and need. This time we were both breathless.

We sat looking at each other for a minute. "I should go." He nodded in agreement and got out of the car. I opened my door and got out as well. I had already retrieved my car keys and started walking over to my car. He

followed me and waited while I unlocked the door of my

car. He opened it for me and I got in.

"Will you come over next Saturday and let me cook

for you?"

"Yes, I would like that."

He smiled, leaned over and gave me a quick kiss

good bye. "I will see you next Saturday then." He closed

the door and I started up the car.

All of the way home I was wondering what I was

doing. Going to his house would be dangerous if I didn't

want this to go further. Do I want this to go further? Is this

as good as it gets? He seems to really feel something for

me; do I feel as excited about him? He is good looking; he is nice to me, employed, and funny. What's not to like or be attracted to? When I got home I went to bed exhausted but thinking about Tim. My thoughts then drifted to Tony. What did Kate mean that I don't see him? I will be glad when school starts and I don't have time for all of this drama. I will talk to Tammy about all of this tomorrow. She will help me gain some perspective.

The next morning I sent Tammy a text.

"Want to go to dinner with me and my parents tonight for my birthday. I need to talk to you. Girl stuff."

Happy Birthday girl friend. I have a date with Mike tonight. How was your date with Tim? Is everything okay?

Thanks, and everything is fine.

Did you go to his place after dinner, lol?

Only to get my car.

What's up with that?

What do you mean?

He didn't invite you in for a happy birthday romp?

NO! God your gross. Go romp with Mike.

Oh I will every chance I get.

I stopped answering. She is out of control.

About mid afternoon my mom knocked on my door. She came in holding a vase of red roses. These came for you.

I sat up and took the vase from her. The card wished me a happy birthday from Tim. My mom watched me with a glowing smile.

"It must have been a good date."

"Yeah, it was."

My mom left the room with a little bounce in her step. I am sure she is already planning the wedding. I would almost prefer a parent who wants me to just concentrate on school.

Chapter 7

As the week plugged along I watched Tony trying to figure out what I wasn't seeing. I never did get to talk to Tammy about this issue since her every waking moment was now being spent with Mike. Tony was his usual self, confident, friendly and fun. I see Tony just fine. I don't know what Kate is talking about. I continued to concentrate on my work and put the worry out of my mind.

Saturday was here and I was getting ready to go to Tim's house. I didn't want my parents to know that I was going there so I told them that I was going out with Tammy. They would panic if they knew that I was going a boy's house that was much older than me. Actually, a man's house not a boy. I drove threw town until I reached his townhouse. I was praying that Greg wouldn't be there. He is a pompous loud mouth and it would ruin my night if he was there hanging out with us. I pulled into the driveway and cursed when I saw Greg's car parked there. I got out and walked to the door. Thankfully Tim answered. He looked at me and smiled.

"Come in."

I stepped in and nervously looked around. I didn't see Greg anywhere. Tim took my hand and led me in. "I am making teriyaki chicken with rice and corn on the cob. I hope that you like it."

"Sounds good. I am starving."

Tim smiled and offered me a glass of Pinot Grigio. I took a sip and then I heard voices coming down the hall. It was Greg and a woman. They were laughing and bantering about something and then they entered the kitchen and stopped as if they were surprised to see someone there. Greg smiled a sleezy grin and said, "Aren't you the girl that's at the Arizona Air counter?"

I nodded affirmative.

Tim then introduced Yvette. "Isabella this is Yvette. Yvette, Isabella."

I didn't try to shake her hand because she was busy pulling her hair back into a hair tie. "Hi, it's nice to meet you."

She grinned, "Yeah honey, it's nice to meet you too."

I couldn't help but to think that Yvette looked rough, like she had been road hard over the years. She reminded me of Cha Cha from Grease, frizzy unmanageable hair, big boobs and tight clothes. She was definitely Greg's type.

"We are heading over to Yvette's for the night. You kids have fun." Greg spat out. He then draped his arm around Yvette's shoulders and they walked out. We just watched, as they left not commenting further. Once they were gone I turned my attention back to Tim. He had already busied himself with food preparation.

"Do you need any help?"

He grinned, "No, this is a piece of cake."

We sat on the back patio and enjoyed dinner and half a bottle of wine. Tim picked up our dishes and then turned on some music. He came out and took me by the hand. "Dance with me."

I got up and followed him inside. He took my hand

in his and I felt the other on my waist. We danced slowly to

a country song in the living room. It wasn't anything that I

would typically listen to but he seemed to like it. He

cradled his face in my neck and I felt him gently kiss it. His

hands slid to my sides and he pulled me closer. My heart

was already beating faster, I think mostly from being

nervous. He nuzzled my neck and worked his way up to my

lips. We had stopped dancing as we stood there in the

living room. He started leading me backwards while

kissing me and I realized we were heading to his room. He

pushed the door open and we went inside. He left the lights

off and kicked the door closed behind him. My heart was

racing and I felt apprehension. Did I want to do this? He

continued to lead me backwards and I felt the bed behind

my legs. We stood kissing and embracing and he laid me

back on the bed. He laid on me while his kiss got harder

and more urgent. I felt his hands under my shirt as they

moved up and caressed my nipples through my bra. He

then pulled it down and I felt him squeeze my nipple. I

gasped not expecting the surge that went through me. He

caressed me and kissed me more. My breathing was hard

already but I didn't know what to do. His hand then moved

lower and I felt him pull up my dress. He then pulled away

from my mouth and whispered into my ear, "Are you on

birth control?"

I didn't expect that. Didn't all men carry condoms with them? I shook my head no.

"You need to do something about that, okay?"

I shook my head yes, still breathing hard and trying to control myself. His lips returned to me, and his hand continued to travel lower. I felt his fingers inside my panties and then touch me softly. I gasped at the pleasure that surged through me, unable to contain myself. He caressed me slowly and I was coming unglued already. He then slid his finger in me and moved it rhythmically back and forth.

"Oh baby you are so tight. Have you done this before?"

"Only once."

He paused just for a moment and met my eyes. Then he moved in me with more determination. I was meeting his movements as if to beg for more. He didn't stop and began moving faster while his thumb caressed me simultaneously. He then put his mouth on my nipple and sucked and pulled. That was it, I arched and shook as a deep groan came from me. I had never felt like this and couldn't control what was happening to me. I then reached a climax that made me gasp and groan like a harlot. Tim looked up at me and smiled his finger still in me. Ah, yes, that's it, this is the magic of the phalanges. I laughed and was embarrassed.

"This is going to get better every time, you will

see."

Better? Seriously? I could die if it gets better. I just

smiled and nodded at him in agreement. We laid together

for a couple of hours as I drifted off to sleep. I woke some

time later, startled knowing that I needed to get home.

"I have to go."

Tim opened his eyes and nodded. "Okay, I will

walk you out."

We got up and I gathered my shoes and purse. We

went out into the living room and made our way to the

door. I was thankful that Greg and Yvette hadn't returned. I

don't think I could have endured walking past them

knowing what we were just doing in Tim's room. He

walked me out to my car. It was late, almost midnight. He

leaned down and kissed me.

"Good night Isabella. Drive safe."

"Good night. Thank you for such a nice evening."

He smiled, "Oh you are welcome."

I flushed and was glad that it was dark. I got into

my car and made my way home and to my own bed.

When morning came I called Tammy. No answer. I

left her a message. "Hey girlfriend, long time, no talk.

Monday is registration for classes. I am going to do it all

online but I was going to go to campus to pick up books. I

thought maybe we could go together and check out the

campus. Let me know."

I hung up disappointed and missing my friend.

Hopefully she would call later.

Chapter 8

On Monday morning I awoke and logged onto my computer to enroll in my classes. I had asked for today off in order to get enrolled and ready for fall classes. I hadn't heard from Tammy. I hoped everything was okay with her. It took me about an hour to get it all completed. I printed off the list of books I needed and got ready to go. As I pulled into the parking lot my phone rang. It was Tammy.

"Hey, where have you been? I was hoping that we would be doing the college campus thing together today."

There was a pause before Tammy answered. "Isabella, I am going to wait a semester before I go back to school."

"What? Why? Do your parents know?"

"No, I haven't told them yet. Mike is certain that they are going to offer me a position and I would like to work for a while and save some money before diving back into academia."

"Tammy, are you sure about this? You know that it's hard to go back once you take a break. They warned about this in school. Remember?"

"I know, I know, but I just need the space and independence right now. It will be okay. I promise."

"Is this because of Mike? Did he talk you out of school?"

"Gosh Isabella, am I talking to my mother right now or my friend?" Tammy snapped back.

I was stunned that she had just lashed out at me. I tried not to let on that this really bothered me. "I am just concerned for you, that's all, and I am disappointed that we won't be doing this together."

"I know. I am sorry too, but it is what I want to do for now. Please understand."

I sighed heavily. "What happens if you don't get a job offer at Union Air? What then?" I spoke softly this time.

"I don't know. Apply at another airline I guess. At least now I will have experience."

I was silent for a minute before saying anything else. "So, what are you doing today?"

"I am going to Mikes to hang out."

I said nothing.

"Maybe we could all get together and go out sometime soon?"

"Yeah, that'll be fun. I'll tell Tim to get with Mike."

"How are things going with Tim?"

"Fine." I no longer felt like discussing my relationship with her or anything else for that matter. I don't know why I felt so mad at her. It is her life and if she

doesn't want to go to school then so be it. Why do I care?

"Good, I am glad. I will see you at work during the

week."

"Okay, bye."

"Bye."

I hung up and looked out my car window for a

moment. This sucked. I missed my friend and was bitter

that Mike has taken her from me. I then got out of the car

and made way onto campus. It was bigger then I

anticipated but I found my way around with relative ease.

The campus looks down on the city and backs up to the

Tucson Mountains. I entered the bookstore and started

going down my list. I looked up briefly when I heard an

explosion of laughter coming from the end of the aisle

where I was searching for Positioning 101. I saw a group of

4 college boys laughing hysterically about something. As I

glanced down the aisle I caught the eye of one of them. He

was Hispanic, with brood shoulders, thick muscular arms,

deep brown eyes and his head was shaved bald. His facial

hair ran down his jaw line and ended at his chin and up to

his bottom lip in a line. He had a large tribal looking tattoo

on his upper arm that accentuated his muscular arms. His

smile was infectious and I found myself smiling just

looking at him. I caught myself and looked away quickly.

How embarrassing. I continued on with my book search

and then got in line to pay. As I stood there I glanced one more time in the direction of the mysterious man with the infectious smile. I didn't see him there anymore and was surprised that I felt disappointed. I paid and walked out toward my car. I looked around as I walked hoping to spot him. I saw him again as he was getting into his white, Silverado truck. The truck was as well kept as him, spotless, expensive rims, and dark windows. He didn't see me this time but I definitely saw him. He slid behind the wheel and started it up. Music in Spanish came bellowing out from within. He pulled out and left. I smiled again for no apparent reason as I walked to my car.

Chapter 9

The next few weeks were like the weeks before. I

worked, hung out with Tony and went out with Tim one

night each weekend. I could tell that Tim wanted more

from me and I remembered him saying he wanted me to get

on birth control. He was probably right. It would be a smart

thing to do. How was I going to do this without my parents

knowing? Maybe I could just go to Planned Parenthood.

Then my parents will never know. I searched my phone for

the number and made an appointment. I was scared. I

missed Tammy and wished that she would come with me

but we hadn't hung out at all for weeks now.

It was my last week of my internship and Tony and

I were working together at the gate today. We were in

between flights and enjoying the reprieve of passengers for

the moment.

"So Friday is your last day?"

I nodded affirmative.

"When does school start?

"On Monday?"

"Are you excited?"

"Yeah, I guess. A little nervous too."

He smiled genuinely. "It's going to be fun Bella. Just promise me that you will keep in touch."

"I will Tony. I could never just walk away from you."

He smiled warmly. "And don't sell yourself short okay? You never think you are worthy of achieving greatness, but you can. Just believe in yourself okay?"

"I will. Don't worry, really."

"Wanna go cruising on Friday night?" He said with a smile.

"You finished it!" I nearly shouted.

He nodded yes.

"Yes! Yes! I would love to go cruising." I was so excited.

"Let's go have dinner at *Mi Casa* and then we'll take her out on a cruise."

"It's a date." I felt so happy at that moment. He was the only close friend I had right now and I cherished it.

We worked two more flights and then my shift was over. I was walking to my car when I heard Tammy call my name from behind me. I stopped and turned around and she came running up.

"Hey there." She said as she gave me a hug.

"Hi." I said flatly, still annoyed that she hasn't been in touch as promised.

"I just got offered a ground crew position at Union Air! Isn't that great?"

"Yeah, that's awesome. What does it mean to be ground crew?"

"I will be working outside loading the planes, flagging them in, you know, ground crew."

"Didn't you want counter or gate?"

"This is where you have to start. I thought you would be happy for me?"

"I am happy for you, I just wanted you to get the position you wanted that's all."

"Well I did. I got a position at Union Air and that's what I wanted." She said snippy.

"And I am happy for you." I said again as I turned and continued walking.

Tammy didn't say anything more nor did she choose to walk any further with me. I walked to my car and didn't look back. We were so distant ~~anymore~~ now that I wasn't sure that we were even still friends.

Friday came before I knew it. I was looking forward to dinner and a cruise down Speedway with Tony. I was feeling a little sad that I wasn't offered a permanent position at Arizona Air but there wasn't anything available right now. I would probably have to wait tables or

something through school. I was most bothered about

leaving Tony. I looked forward to the days that we would

work together. We met at *Mi Casa* and were seated for

dinner. I loved the Mexican food here. It was fantastic. I

ordered enchiladas and a soda and Tony took the special.

"I have some news that I want to share with you."
Tony declared excitedly.

I smiled. "Okay, what is it?"

"I am transferring up to Seattle. I will finish school

there and try to get a job with corporate after graduation."

I tried not to let my eyes fill with tears but I

couldn't help it. My sole friend was leaving. I pasted on a

smile anyway and said, "I am so happy for you. When do you leave?"

"In two weeks. I wanted to give Marcia at least a little time to replace me. Why don't you ask her if you could take my position?"

A tear rolled down my cheek as I shook my head no. "No, I will be too busy with school to work full time." I paused for a moment and then said, "I will really miss you."

"I will miss you too." Tony said with sadness on his face.

I wiped away my tear and forced the smile back on my face. "Have you found a place to live up there yet?"

"Yes, the school has apartments that it rents out for upper classmen. They aren't bad."

"Well, we should celebrate." I raised my soda glass to his. "Cheers and good luck." I clanked my glass to his.

"Cheers and thank you." Tony said. "You should come visit me sometime."

"I would like that."

We ate and went to his remodeled truck. It was beautiful. Shiny rims, new yellow paint job. The truck was hot. He smiled brightly as he showed me all of the features of his prized possession. We got in and headed for Speedway. We rolled the windows down and drove slow. We turned on the stereo and enjoyed just cruising around.

Girls would lean out of their cars and shout to Tony as we

drove by and we just laughed and kept going. We drove

back and forth at least a dozen times before we decided to

call it a night. Tony drove me back to my car. When we got

there he turned off the truck and just looked at me before

we got out. "Thank you for cruising with me tonight."

I laughed. "You are welcome. It was fun."

We sat for a moment longer saying nothing. "How

are things going with Tim?"

"Fine." I shrugged my shoulders.

He said nothing and just stared at me. "I am glad

that everything is good."

I looked down at my hands saying nothing.

"Bella. If you ever need anything you know how to get ahold of me."

"I know. And the same goes for you."

He smiled and leaned over and kissed my cheek. I got out and he walked over to my car to open the door for me.

"Good night Bella."

"Good night Tony. Thank you again for taking me cruising. I had a lot of fun."

"Thank you for going with me."

I gave him a hug and leaned up to kiss him on the cheek. I turned and got into my car. I cried all of the way home and I didn't know why. This was stupid. Why couldn't I be happy for the people around me? I crawled

into bed with swollen eyes still blubbering and fell asleep.

Chapter 10

Saturday morning my phone rang. "Hello?"

"It's me." Tim said.

"Hi you."

"Are you doing anything this weekend?"

"Not really, why?"

"Want to go to Vegas?"

"Want, yes, but I don't have the money to run off to

Vegas."

"You only need a little gambling money, the rest is on me."

"Tim, I can't let you spend that kind of money on me, and besides I have class on Monday. I need to be back and rested."

"I have a buddy pass for the flight and a poker room rate from my dad at the casino. I will have you home in time for school."

I was silent, trying to decide if this was a good idea. "When are you coming home?

"Sunday afternoon. Plenty of time to rest. Come on Isabella, it will be fun."

"Are you sure it's not too much?"

"I am sure, just say you'll come."

"When do we leave?"

"Be here in two hours."

I snapped my phone closed and headed for the shower. How was I going to tell my parents that I was going to Vegas with Tim? I won't. I will tell them that I am going with Tammy. I will say that she gets passes now that she works for the airlines. I showered and packed in less than an hour. I walked out with my carryon bag and met my mom in the kitchen. "Hey mom. Tammy invited me to Vegas this weekend now that she gets free fights. I will be home Sunday."

She frowned slightly. "You're not old enough to go to Vegas."

"Sure I am. There are lots of shows and entertainment that you don't need to be 21 to do."

"Where are you staying?"

"Um. I don't know. I didn't ask her. I will text you when I get there and let you know."

"Are you going to be home with plenty of time so you don't miss the first day of classes?"

"Yes mom. I know when school is okay?"

"Okay, okay, be safe."

"Thanks mom." I leaned over and gave her a kiss.

I drove to Tim's with anticipation and very nervous. This means that we will be spending the night together. We have never done that. I have never been to Vegas either. I hope I can get away with playing some slots or something while I am there. I pulled into Tim's driveway and he met me at the door. "You ready?'

"Yep."

He smiled and kissed me tenderly. "Then let's get out of here."

It felt weird walking through the airport in street clothes and waving at my old work friends. It was even more awkward seeing Tony and waving as I walked by with Tim. I felt like I was cheating on him or something. It was absurd but it was how I felt nonetheless. Tammy was

at the gate and Tim stepped behind the counter to check us

in.

"Where are you two going?" She asked with a sly

grin.

"Vegas." Tim said without even looking up at her.

She continued to grin at me like I was doing

something that I shouldn't be. "Well, don't do anything too

crazy. What happens in Vegas should stay in Vegas you

know."

Tim looked at her and rolled his eyes. "Don't worry

Tammy, I think we can handle it." He walked out from

behind the counter and grabbed my hand and led me to

some far chairs to sit and wait. He looked annoyed with

Tammy, which surprised me. We boarded about a half an

hour later. The flight was short from Tucson and before I

knew it we were hailing a cab to take us to the casino. Tim

checked us in under the poker room guest rate. His dad

played poker there daily and was a major contender in the

Super Bowl of Poker held yearly in Vegas. I was certain

that I was finally going to meet the legend this weekend.

Tim got our keys and led me up to the room. It was

beautiful with dark wood furniture, color-strewn linens and

cool metal accents. We dropped our bags in the closet and

Tim called for a bottle of wine to be brought to the room.

We sat on the patio and drank the cool bottle of Pinot. I was feeling tipsy and much braver. Tim leaned over and gave me a long, sensual kiss. "Let's go play."

I nodded in agreement but was hoping that nobody would card me. He grabbed my hand and led me to the door. He grabbed his phone as the door closed behind us and made a call. By the time we were leaving the elevator an older gentleman with slicked back hair and a slight limp approached us. Tim shook his hand and gave him a hug. "Dad, this is Isabella. It is her first time to Vegas."

He smiled and shook my hand. "It's nice to meet you." He said loudly.

"It's nice to meet you too." I said suddenly feeling very nervous. Is this who he was on the phone with on our way down?

His dad turned and started walking and we followed behind him. "Hey, Bobby, these are my kids."

Bobby was standing at the entrance to the poker room. He nodded politely. Tim's dad turned and shoved some money in Tim's hand. "Why don't you kids get something to eat?" He turned and walked back into the poker room. I couldn't help but to feel like the introduction to Bobby was intentional, but didn't know why. We then went to California Pizza and ate.

"Are you ready to hit the tables?"

"No. I don't even know how to play. I will stand

behind you and watch for now."

"Are you sure? It's fun."

"I will watch and try not to get thrown out."

We walked around until Tim found a table he liked.

He sat down with his chips and I stood watching. He lost

the first hand but won the next two. The waitress came

around and Tim ordered both of us drinks and threw a chip

on her tray. We were there for about 2 hours before Tim

called in quits. He was up about $100. We left the casino

and walked the strip. We walked in and out of the casinos

playing here and there. I was keeping a low profile and Tim

did most of the playing. Time flew by and before I knew it,

it was 2am. "Let's go back to the room." Tim whispered in

my ear. I was totally tipsy from drinking all night. I nodded

and said ok. We made our way to the room and went in.

The door had barely closed and Tim had grabbed me by the

waist and pulled me to him hard. He began kissing me. As

his lips were pressing on mine, his tongue moved into my

mouth urging me for more. He held me to him tightly and

continued to kiss me as his hands held onto my waist. He

then started moving me toward the bed. My heart was

beating fast and I was not hesitating to move with him. His

hands pulled my shirt out of my jeans and he pulled it over

my head. I stood panting as is hands returned to my waist

and he kissed me some more. He took off his shirt and

pressed against me. I moaned at feeling our skin against

each other. He grabbed my hand and put it against him. I

could feel how hard he was and I wanted to make him feel

as good as he always makes me feel. He took my hand and

rubbed it against him through his jeans. It made my

breathing quicken even more. I kept touching him as he

unbuttoned my jeans and slid them down. I stepped out of

them now just in my panties and bra. I tried to unbutton his

jeans but was nervous and kept fumbling. He reached down

and unbuttoned his jeans and I slid them down to the floor.

I put my hands on him again and he groaned. He laid me

down on the bed and began kissing me down my neck,

between my breasts, lower to my belly button. I was

gasping now not knowing what was coming, he pulled

down my panties and grabbed my leg and pulled it to the

side. I felt his lips on me and then his tongue in me. I

screamed out not expecting this and oh my goodness it felt

so good. His tongue moved in and out and his hand began

to caress me in a way that was going to make me explode. I

am groaning so loud now that I was sure that the entire

casino could hear me. He kept going moving faster now

and I could feel the tension building. I couldn't take it

anymore. I reached down and grabbed his head, oh my God

I am going to explode. He knew I was close and kept

licking and tasting me until I let go into an erratic screech

of desire and came into his mouth. He groaned with

pleasure and looked up at me and smiled. He licked his way

up to my breasts and reached behind me and undid my bra.

Pulling it off of me his sucked on each nipple gently. Then

he made his way up to the nape of my neck and kissed me

gently. Just as my breathing was returning to normal he

pulled off his boxers and climbed between my legs. He

lifted each leg up over his shoulder and I was scared of

what was coming next. He eased into me and I was so wet

that I almost came again at just him entering into me. I

arched up and groaned. "Oh yes baby, you are so wet, I

love it." He started to move slowly but increased quickly as

we both moved rhythmically together. He was ready to

come but I wasn't sure if I could yet. He let lose with a cry

and I didn't know what to do. I expected to feel the same
intensity that I did before but I didn't. He collapsed onto
me and our breathing evened. We lay together for several
minutes before I felt him fall asleep. I slid out from beneath
him and turned on my side. Maybe that is what it is like for
everyone. I really liked it when he kissed me down there
though. That was great. I fell asleep with Tim for the first
time, the first time that I had ever spent the entire night
with a man.

The morning came quickly and I felt uncomfortable
waking up naked. The room was bright and I looked around
trying to find my clothes. I stumbled to the bathroom with a

throbbing headache from drinking too much the night

before. Tim was still sleeping soundly and I slipped into the

shower. The shower felt wonderful after a night of drinking

and having sex. I was still worried about my lack of follow

through. What the hell was wrong with me? Tim is

everything women want. I just needed more experience. It

will come with time. I finished up and got ready. Tim was

awake and drinking coffee when I came out of the

bathroom. He smiled and said good morning.

"Good morning yourself. How do you feel?"

"I am fine. I am not the one who drank all night."

I stood stunned. Did I really drink that much last

night? Wasn't he drinking too? "I didn't drink *all* night."

"I am gonna jump in the shower. My dad wants to take us to breakfast before we go." He got up and went to the bathroom. I couldn't help but to feel bad like I had embarrassed him last night. Had I drank too much? Why am I overthinking this?

An hour later we had checked out and were having breakfast with his dad at Caesar's Palace. It seemed like no matter where we went his dad knew someone and it seemed like everyone owed him something. He either got free meals or free drinks. He never explained but accepted without batting an eye. I thanked him for breakfast and we grabbed a cab to the airport. I had been pretty quiet all morning worrying about my alcohol intake and if the sex was good enough for Tim. He was a lot older than me and a

lot more experienced. Would he want to be with me again

or did this not meet his expectations?

I slept the entire flight, and before I knew it we

were landing back in Tucson. Tim took my hand as we

walked through the airport making our way out to the car.

We were both quiet and I wondered what he was thinking

about. We drove to his house in the same silence and I

decided that we were both exhausted. When we got to

Tim's I asked if I could run inside to use the bathroom

before driving home. Tim opened the door for us and we

could hear yelling coming from the other side of the house.

I assumed it was Greg and Yvette since their cars were

outside. I couldn't hear what it was about but it sounded

angry. I made my way to Tim's bedroom because he had

his own bathroom. Tim acted like he didn't hear a thing. I

came out when I was done and heard Greg and Yvette

yelling in the living area. She was crying and he was telling

her to go. She turned and left slamming the door behind

her. I continued to stand in Tim's room not wanting to go

out there. After the door closed I heard Tim ask him what

that was all about.

"That lying little bitch is pregnant and is claiming

that it is mine."

"Dude I am sorry. How does she know if it is yours?"

I couldn't believe my ears. Why wouldn't it be his? What makes him think that she has been with anyone else?

"That's what I asked her and she went ape shit on me. I just fucking told her that I don't want or need a kid so get rid of it."

"Is she going to?"

"How the fuck do I know. She got all emotional and started crying, claiming that she loves me and shit. You know, she was supposed to be on birth control so I would love to know how the fuck this happened."

"Did you ask her about that?"

"Yeah, she forgot to take it a couple of times and now this is my issue to deal with apparently."

I stood in Tim's room listening not believing what I was hearing. Were they really blaming all of this on her? I couldn't believe that Tim was standing there condoning Greg's demand to have her abort her pregnancy. I just wanted to get out of here. I was starting to feel sick. I slowly walked through Tim's door. Greg's head shot around when he heard me. "Where the hell did you come from?"

My face went white. "I came in with Tim. I had to use the bathroom."

"Did you just hear everything that I said?"

I nodded yes.

"You better keep your mouth shut especially when it comes to your little friend Tammy. She will be blabbing my business all over the airport."

I kept waiting for Tim to say something, to tell Greg to back off, but he didn't. "I won't say anything." Was all I could seem to say at this point.

"Whatever." Greg shot back and then went back upstairs to his room slamming the door.

I just looked over at Tim waiting for him to say something. When he remained silent I turned and walked to the door. He followed me as I went outside to get my bag and drive home. I opened my car hastily and I threw my bag in the car. Right before I got in Tim grabbed my arm and pulled me to him for a hug. "You are on birth control right?"

I pushed away and looked at him. "Yeah Tim and I even take it everyday. Don't worry, that won't be you." I was very short and to the point. I then got in my car and drove home. Before I got out of the car I shot a text to Tammy.

I told my mom that I went to Vegas with you. Hope you will cover me.

I got no response so I got out and went into my house. I needed to get some sleep before I started school in the morning.

Chapter 11

When I got to campus I found myself scouring the parking lot for a White Silverado truck. How ridiculous was that. This is a huge campus and the chance of seeing the Latin mystery man was slim and none. I had two classes twice a week and then externship at an assigned hospital twice a week for two years. You are basically with the same the class throughout the program since it is so structured. Today's classes were Radiography 1 and Medical Terminology. I found my first class and went inside to take a seat. I found my way to the middle of the room. Not too far in front and not in the back. I have a theory that this is the safest place in the classroom. Once I took my seat I flipped open my phone to make sure that I had silenced it. I hadn't heard from Tim since I left yesterday. I felt sad as I thought about the events of the last 48 hours. Suddenly a text came in. It was from Tony.

"Good luck with your first day of classes. You will do great. I would love to hear about your day if you have time later."

With a smile on my face I replied. *"Thank you and I will call you later."* What was I going to do without him?

My thoughts were interrupted by a girl who had taken the seat next to me. "Hi."

"Hi."

"My name is Jody."

"It's nice to meet you, my name is Isabella."

Jody had long black curly hair. Her skin was very white for having such dark hair and I wondered if she colored it that color or if it was natural. She wore red lipstick which contrasted against her fair skin and dark hair.

My thoughts were interrupted when the professor came in and started class. The next hour and a half went quickly and was mostly focused on the syllabus

. When class was done I was off to the next location for Medical Terminology.

"What's your next class?" I heard Jody ask.

"Um, Medical Terminology."

"Me too. Mind if I walk with you?"

"Sure."

We wandered out and started negotiating the campus looking for the next classroom. I was kind of glad to have someone with me since I was unsure about where to go.

"I think it is in the Basic Science's building."

I looked at my map of the campus and agreed. "I think you're right. Don't they have an App for this or something?"

Jody laughed. "I know, right? There's an App for everything else, why not campus maps? You should market it and retire now."

I laughed at her whit. It was refreshing to be around someone so light at heart.

"I just moved here from Pittsburg and I live and die by my google maps."

"What brought you to Tucson?"

"My dad moved here about a year ago after my parents divorced. I thought it would be nice to get out of the snow."

"I am from Rochester, I know what you mean."

"Rochester Minnesota?"

"New York."

"Buffalo Bills country."

I laughed and nodded affirmative. "Oh yeah. The Bills versus the Steelers is the best game of the season."

As we rounded the corner almost to our next destination I stopped cold in my tracks. There he was. Jody was still walking and talking and didn't notice that I had stopped.

"H e l l o, where'd you go?" She stopped and turned around.

There he was sauntering down the sidewalk. He had on aviator glasses, faded jeans that hung on hips just right and a cream colored button up linen shirt that was a little

snug to accent his build. Jody looked over to see what I was

looking at when a little brunette bounced up to him and put

herself under his arm. She was perfect, tiny, not over 5 feet

tall, thin, beautiful long dark hair with carefully placed

curls on the ends. She was wearing designer short, shorts

and a tank top. She had lovely dark, smooth skin. Of course

she was with this perfect man.

"Now that is delicious eye candy." I heard Jody say.

I nodded and didn't say anything. What was there to

say? That I saw him once before and have a secret

infatuation with him? We kept walking and found our class.

"This week is going to be long and painful reviewing the syllabus for every class. You would think that they would just email that out prior to class so that we could get down to business on the first day." Jody complained.

"Now that is a good idea that *you* should market." We both laughed. It was nice to talk to a girl for once.

"Where are you off to after class?" Jody inquired.

"I was going to get a bite to eat and then apply for some jobs."

"Where are you going to apply?

"I was considering Patty's. Do you know where that is? The one over on Broadway."

"No, I have never been there."

"Do you wanna come with me?"

"Sure. I have nothing to do but go home."

After class we headed over to Patty's and had burgers. Jody was funny and carefree. I liked being around her. Before we left I stopped and asked if they were hiring. The bartender said that they were and made a call to the back so that I could talk to the manager. I wasn't expecting that and wished that I had dressed nicer. The manager came out and shook hands. "I'm Pam. So I hear you girls are looking for a job. Do you have any experience waiting tables?"

"Ah, no. I just finished an internship with Arizona Airlines, but I really don't have any other work experience." Pam just looked at me. She was intimidating, tall, wider shoulders than most men and strait, shoulder length hair. Her white t-shirt and faded blue jeans were far too tight.

"How 'bout you?" Pam said to Jody.

"Well, I waited tables at Denny's in Pittsburg before I moved here."

Pam continued to look at us. "How old are you two?"

"Nineteen." We said in unison.

I heard the bartender chuckle and walk to the other end of the bar.

"I need help on Friday nights right now. The menu is pretty basic and I will have Michelle train you two. Can you start next week?"

We both nodded in agreement.

"Let's have you fill out the application and the tax forms. You will need to buy a Patty's t-shirt and we will supply an apron."

We sat in a booth and filled out our paper work. "Isabella, is it okay with you that I work here too? I know you came in here to get a job and I can look somewhere else if you want."

"Don't be silly. It will be fun."

She smiled and kept filling in her paperwork. We handed it all in to Pam and collected our t-shirts. We are to be here by 4:00 next Friday. Jody and I exchanged numbers and agreed that we would meet up at school the next day. I drove home feeling lighter then I did earlier this morning. When I got home I called Tony.

"Hey Bella. How was the first day?'

"It was fabulous of course"

We both laughed.

"Fabulous?"

"Well considering it is syllabus week it was good. Next week will be better when we dive into the classes and get our hospital assignments. I also managed to find a job

after work."

"Really? Where at?"

"Patty's Bar and Grill."

"Really? Doing what?"

"Waiting tables on Friday nights. Jody will be

working there too."

"Who is Jody?"

"A girl I met at school today. She seems cool. She's

from Pittsburg."

"A new friend and job all in one day. It sounds like

a good day." We were silent for just a moment when he

asked, "So how was Vegas?"

My heart dropped. I already felt guilty about going there with Tim, and for traipsing in front of Tony, which shouldn't matter because we are just friends.

"It was fun. There was a lot to do and see there."

"I am glad you had fun."

"It was fun until we got home anyway."

"Why, what happened when you got home?"

I don't know why I even brought it up. Was it because it was still bothering me or because I wanted Tony's take on things? Tony was leaving anyway so it doesn't really matter if he knows. "When we got back to Tim's house Greg and Yvette were having a knock down drag out fight."

Tony said nothing so I kept talking.

"Yvette told Greg that she was pregnant and Greg imploded on her, wanting to know if it was his and then told her to get rid of it. Can you believe that? Why would he question if it was his and who does he think he is telling her to get rid of it?"

"What did Tim say during about all of this?"

"Nothing. That's just it, he said nothing."

"Why do you think that is?"

"I have no idea. I was disappointed that he wasn't trying to talk some sense into Greg."

"Bella, don't get mad at me for saying this, but would it be outside the box for Greg to consider that the baby wasn't his?"

"What do you mean?"

"Do you know Yvette?"

"Not really."

"Let's just say her reputation is colorful."

"Oh." I felt my face getting red. Thank goodness we were just talking on the phone.

"However, demanding that she abort her pregnancy is ludicrous. What did she say?"

"She just left crying."

"Well that sounds like a hot mess."

"No kidding. I am glad that's not me."

We stayed silent on the phone for a moment knowing that this could be me if I wasn't careful. Tony changed the subject.

"Maybe I could come in to Patty's and have my last meal in Tucson with you?"

My heart dropped knowing that was coming soon. "I would like that."

"Then it's a date. Good night Bella."

"Good night." I said as I hung up the phone. No more than a minute later my phone buzzed. It was a text from Tammy.

How was Vegas?

Fun, lot's to do.

Did you hear that Yvette is pregnant?

Well, good news travels fast doesn't it? *Yes, I*
heard. Boy did I hear, I thought to myself.

She is totally trash talking Greg. I guess he's being
a jerk about it.

If she only knew. *Really?*

Yeah. He actually asked her if it was his. Can you
believe that?

Wow. Was all I said.

I miss seeing you at the airport.

Me too.

Did you start school today?

Yes.

And?

It was fine. You know how the first week goes.
Actually she doesn't, because she isn't going to go to
school, I thought to myself.

Cool. Mike and I are going to the APP Friday after
work. Do want to meet us?

Can't. Got to work.

Work? Where?

Patty's on Broadway.

That's awesome. Maybe we can come in sometime
and sit in your section?

Yeah. That would be fun.

We went silent after that and I felt sad because I missed my old friend. I hope she would come around soon and not be quite so connected to Mike.

Chapter 12

I didn't hear from Tim until Thursday night. I was short and irritated by then. Why hasn't he called before now?

"How's the first week of school going?"

"Fine." Was all I could spat out.

"Just fine?"

"Yep."

"Are you mad?"

"A little."

"Why?"

"Why haven't you called since our Vegas trip?"

"Why haven't you called? I was trying to give you space knowing that you were starting school. What was your excuse?"

His irritation back at me surprised me. Had I hurt his feelings by not calling him? I didn't consider that angle. I decided to change the subject. "How's the anger level in the house with Greg?"

"No anger. They are humping like bunnies again."

"After all of that? What happened to it's not my kid, and get rid of it?"

"I don't know Isabella, I don't ask questions. All I know is that I am not getting any sleep listening to them go at it in the other room."

"Oh. I guess that's good."

He laughed. "Yeah, I guess that is good." We sat silent for a moment. "Tammy said that you got a job at Patty's."

She really is the blabbermouth that Greg says she is. "Yes."

"You know that bar is tough. I am not sure that is a good idea."

I was irritated again. What is he my father now? "I'll be fine."

"I'm serious Isabella"

"I hear you. I will be careful. I promise." There was
an uncomfortable pause. "I should get going and start my
homework since I have to work tomorrow."

"Good night Isa."

"Bye." I hung up still feeling mildly irritated with
his snappy attitude with me. I decided to start my
homework wanting to get ahead. I knew tomorrow was
going to be a long day since I would be working until close.
I was kind of nervous since I had never waited tables
before.

Jody and I went to get something to eat and then get ready for our first day of work. I was still nervous hoping that I wouldn't make a fool out of myself. I wore my new Patty's t-shirt and some black shorts that blended in with my apron. We arrived at the bar early, ready to work and eager to get started. Michelle was thin and tired looking. She was nice enough but definitely not someone you wanted to cross in life. Many of the customers were regulars and she began introducing us to everyone. Before long I had my own section without her help. At about midnight a group of men came in and took the back corner of the bar and one of the pool tables. The people who were already in that area got up and moved or left. I was about to go over there and get drink orders and was shocked to see

the Latin eye candy from school there shooting pool with

his friends. Michelle saw me looking over there and came

up next to me.

"I will take care of Alex and the boys."

"Who's Alex?"

"The one you are standing here drooling over." She

laughed and walked over to them. They all seemed to know

her and she made small talk with them before going to the

bar to get their drinks. Just then he looked up and met my

stare. He grinned to the side and then winked at me. I

immediately pulled my eyes away and made myself busy

with my customers. How embarrassing to be caught staring

again. I wonder where the girlfriend is tonight? They stayed

until close and I noticed that nobody approached them to

challenge them for the pool table or even sat in that area at

all during the night. It was like they owned that corner of

the world. I was cleaning tables and refilling salt and

pepper shakers when they started to make their way out. As

Alex walked by talking to one of his friends he put his hand

on my waist to scoot by me never looking at me or saying

anything. He just kind of moved me out of his way

effortlessly. It didn't matter that I was already occupying

that space. He just removed me from it. In the end it really

didn't matter because the touch of his hand on me was

exciting. I think my heart sped up just for that moment in time and I smiled.

Jody and I counted up our tip money and gave the bartender his cut. All in all, it was a good first night.

Chapter 13

The next week started the same as the week before

and I was grateful for the routine. Tim was frustrated that

we didn't get together on Saturday but I assured him that

we could go out next weekend. I was anxious about today.

Today we were going to get our hospital externship

assignments. I was hoping that me and Jody got the same

location. We were each handed an envelope with our

location and pertinent information such as the manager that

we report to, what hours to report and parking instructions. I opened my envelope. I got Arizona General. They are the best hospital in Tucson, very high tech and affiliated with the University. I looked at Jody. "Where did you get placed?"

"Arizona General."

"Really? Me too!" I started reading the information enclosed. I was reporting to Leah Smith on the day shift on Wednesday and Thursdays. "Did you get days or evenings?"

"Days."

"It's gonna be fun Jody. This is the best hospital in town."

When I got home I called Tony. It was his last week in Tucson and I wanted to share my news with him.

"Hi Bella."

"Guess what?"

"What?"

"I got placed at Arizona General for my clinical externship rotation."

"I take it from your excitement that is good?"

"Yes! They are the best hospital in Tucson. Jody got the same assignment so we can tag team together."

"That is great. I am really happy for you."

"So, last week in Tucson. What's on the agenda?"

"Packing, packing and more packing. I am going to dinner Friday night with this girl I know though."

I felt sad for a minute, then I heard him say, "When do you get a break so we can eat together at Patty's on Friday night?"

"I start at five this week, so come in at nine and I will take a break so we can eat together." I said grinning ear to ear happy to hear the dinner was with me.

"It's a date."

"Okay, I will see you then."

"Friday at nine. See you then."

We hung up and I was sad again. I decided to call Tim. "Hey there."

"Hey. How was your day?"

"It was good. Jody and I got assigned to Arizona General for our clinicals."

"That's great. That was what you were hoping for."

"Yeah, it will be fun." I was silent. I felt sad and I didn't know why.

"Do you want to come over?"

A smile crept over my face. "It's getting late already."

"So come over and stay the night." His voice was sweet and almost sheepish.

"What will I tell my parents?"

"You are nineteen, do they not expect that you will have a boyfriend and maybe even sexual relations?"

My face got red with embarrassment. "I know, but they are traditional and don't feel that you should have sex until after marriage."

"Please come over. I miss you."

That was sweet and made me miss him too. "Okay. I will think of something."

I arrived at Tim's an hour later with a bag packed and my school stuff for the next day. I told my parents that I was staying at Tammy's. I don't know how much longer I was going to be able to get away with that white lie, but for tonight it worked. He met me at the door with a smile. He

grabbed me and pulled me into the house by the hips. He

kicked the door closed behind us and pressed his lips to

mine. His kiss was urgent and hard. We immediately made

our way to his room and he kicked that door closed too. We

fell to the bed still kissing, our hands caressing each other

from top to bottom. He felt his way into my shirt and I felt

his warm hands on my stomach and running up to my bra.

He felt behind me and unclasped it with one hand and

pushed it free. His fingers brushed over my nipples and I

groaned with excitement. I wanted more. I pulled his shirt

up and over his head and let my hands run over his smooth

chest. My breathing was heavy already with anticipation.

He undid his jeans and I pushed them down for him and he kicked them off. His hands were already unbuttoning my jeans and then pulled my pants and panties off. I kicked them off onto the floor. My hands dove into his boxers and I felt his erection. He was hard and he wanted me. I gripped him and began to stroke him back and forth. He groaned and rested his forehead in the nape of my neck as I continued. He moved his head down to my nipple and ran his tongue over it, first kissing it and then running his tongue in a circle around it. His other hand squeezed my other nipple and pulled. The combination made me arch and yell out.

"Oh yeah. I will make you come baby." He pulled

his boxers off and I ran my hand through his pubic hair and

then gripped his balls in my hand gently, with my other

hand I started stroking him again. He closed his eyes and

groaned. I rubbed the wetness coming through on the tip of

his penis. He pulled my hand away and pushed his hand

between my legs. I was wet already and his touch made me

arch in delight. He caressed me and I felt his finger in me

moving in and out. I was panting with anticipation. Then he

grabbed me and flipped me on top of him. I was startled. I

had never been on top and became nervous. He looked at

me with smoldering eyes. "Don't worry. You can do it." He

whispered. He lifted my hips and pushed me down on him.

I felt him slide deep in me. He then grabbed my hips and started moving me up and down on him. My fears went away and I went with his rhythm. I was losing control and began moving faster and faster. I was panting hard. It was coming, I was going to come. He grabbed my hands and kept me upright so I wouldn't lean over him keeping him deep inside of me. I heard his breathing quicken too. "Come on baby, let me have it, let me have you." That was it, I came so hard I yelled out and arched back. He let go and came just when I did. I fell forward exhausted. My breathing still labored. He caressed my back that was sticky from the exertion of our sexual escapade. I felt so good and so tired. I drifted off to sleep and I felt him turn and slip me onto my side. He lay on his side with his arm around me and we fell asleep.

We stayed like that until morning when I woke in a panic. I looked around for a clock afraid that I had missed class. It was 6:00 in the morning; thank goodness my internal alarm got me up in time. I slipped into the shower with Tim still sound asleep. When I was done getting ready I peaked into the bedroom and the bed was empty. Tim must be up. I packed up my bag and headed to the kitchen. The spring in my step slowed a little as I saw Greg and Tim at the counter drinking coffee. I smiled and continued to walk in. Tim smiled and handed me a cup coffee with creamer, just the way I like it. I smiled. "Thank you."

"You're welcome. You ready for class?"

"Yeah, I have to go. Sorry."

"It's okay, I have to work anyway."

Greg stood there smirking at me. My skin was crawling with the way he was looking at me. Where was Yvette? Why isn't he off rubbing her belly or something?

"You coming back tonight?" Greg shot out.

"No, I should go home tonight." I was not sure where this was going and I could tell that Tim wasn't sure either.

"Good, all of that yelling was making me horny and all Yvette wants to do is sleep right now."

My face went red. I couldn't believe he just said that to me. Tim started laughing which made me even madder.

"Shut the hell up. I have heard nothing but you two going at it for a week now." Tim shot back.

"Yeah well the make up sex is over and now she is tired!"

I just turned around and started walking toward the door. He is the most vile man I have ever met. I do not understand why Tim shares a place with him. I could hear Tim walking behind me. We stepped outside. "Hey Isabella." He grabbed my arm, "Don't let him get to you. He is just an ass. He does it more when he knows it bothers you." He pulled me close to him and said, "Thank you for

staying over with me. It was great." I leaned my forehead

against his chest and he hugged me. "Isabella?"

"Yeah?" My head was still resting on his chest and I

was looking at the ground.

"I think I am falling in love with you."

I was stunned. Is this what love felt like? Everyone

told me there was no doubt when you felt it. You would

know when you found the right person. Maybe this was it.

He was good to me. He takes me out, took me to Vegas,

cares about what I do and that I am safe, and wants me to

stay overnight with him, and that was good too. Maybe this

is what people are talking about. "I love you too." I heard

myself say. He smiled down at me and now I looked up at him and smiled back. He leaned down and kissed me softly. "I should get going to school though."

He laughed and nodded in agreement. "Okay, have a good day."

"Thanks. I will call you after school."

"Okay, I will be waiting."

I went to class with a bounce in my step. Jody was already inside. "Hey girlfriend." I said as I sat down next to her.

"Hi, good night?"

I looked puzzled at her. Could she tell that I had been with Tim? Did I look different somehow? "As a matter of fact it was." I smiled.

"I can tell you look happy."

I paused just for a moment and then changed the subject. "Friday my friend Tony is coming in to Patty's to have dinner and say good bye. He is moving to Seattle. I will introduce you to him."

"Is that who you were with last night?"

"No, I just told you, he is my friend."

"Aren't lovers friends too?"

I paused for a minute. Were me and Tim friends or just sex partners? "I guess that is true but I don't have sex with Tony."

"I see." Jody didn't ask who it was that I was having sex with but I am sure she was curious. "I can't wait to start at the hospital tomorrow."

"Me too." Lecture started and we turned our attention to note taking and assignments.

By the time I got home I was exhausted. I went to my room and called Tim like I said I would. "Hi. What are you doing?"

"Hey there. I just got home from work. I am beat."

"Me too."

"Want to come sleep with me?"

"I can't. I really need to get some sleep before I go to clinicals tomorrow."

"That's what I said, come sleep with me." He paused, "Please."

"What am I going to tell my parents?"

"Tell them that you going to go sleep with your boyfriend."

"We've been through this, they don't agree with that kind of behavior."

"Tell them you are staying at Jody's tonight so you can carpool together in the morning."

I thought about that for a minute. "Oh, okay. I will

be there in an hour." My mom didn't seem to be bothered

by me going out for another night so I made a run for it

before she changed her mind. What would she do if she

found out where I was really and that I had lied? I felt

guilty but I had already told Tim that I would be there.

Tim was waiting at the door again for me still in

uniform. I walked in and hugged him ready to drop. He

hugged me back and said, "Come on, let's go lay down." I

nodded in agreement and followed him to his room trailing

behind him while holding his hand. I didn't pay attention to

if Greg's car was here or not. The house seemed quiet

though. He closed his door and shed off the uniform

leaving just his boxers on. I had on a camisole and sport

shorts. He undid the bed and motioned for me to get in with

him. We crawled in and snuggled up together. I was asleep

in a matter of seconds. I awoke several hours later and

looked up at the clock. It was 2:00 in the morning. I wasn't

sure what woke me up until I heard it again. The groaning

and moaning of Greg and Yvette was permeating the house.

Tim awoke and looked at me. "What's wrong?"

"Nothing, I just woke up." Just as I said that the bed

started hitting the wall and Yvette was howling for more.

Tim grinned at me. "You just woke up or you were

awaken?"

"Well I didn't know I had been awaken until I was awake."

Tim rolled onto his side and looked at me and then his hand slid up my leg and rubbed over my panties. I looked at him and shuddered. He kept rubbing back and forth and my breathing was heavy already. He got on top of me and pulled my camisole down so my breasts came out over the top of it. He sucked on each nipple gently at first and then gradually harder. He then bit down gently on one and I unexpectantly gasped. His hand was in my panties caressing me and I was moving against him wanting more. I was panting ready to orgasm when he came over me pushed my panties to the side and pushed into me hard. I yelled out not expecting him so hard. He was ready now

and rammed into me hard again then rapidly. Surprisingly I

was ready too and he felt good inside of me. I was yelling

out each time he came back into me not able to contain how

good it felt. Then I was grabbing his shoulders and

squeezing. I heard myself begging for more and then we

both orgasmed together and Tim yelled as loud as I did. We

went limp and laid together coming down from our high. I

then heard something hit the wall and then Greg yelled,

"Quit showing off!"

I rolled to the side to look at Tim. "You are right, he

is an ass."

Tim laughed and kissed the top of my head. "Just ignore him."

I laid my head back down and we fell back asleep in each other's arms.

Chapter 14

I met Jody in the parking lot of Arizona General.

The place was huge and I was petrified of getting lost in

there. We both had on our school issued navy blue scrubs

that have the school logo on the sleeve. Our school ID

badges were clipped to the shirt pocket. There was no

doubt that we were students. We checked in at the front

desk and were instructed to wait for the preceptor to come

and get us. When Joe arrived he shook our hands and told

us to follow him. He showed us where our lockers were,

issued us lead markers with a tech number on each one.

This way any film that we took was identified by what tech

took it. If there were any questions or feed back on the

finished x-rays they knew exactly who to go to. I

immediately taped mine onto my badge so I wouldn't lose

them. Joe showed us around the department that had ten

diagnostic x-ray rooms, two special procedures labs and

two cardiac cath labs. Down the hall was the CT, MRI and

Ultrasound area. The morning was gone by the time we

went through the tour and looked at the equipment in depth.

We went over the protocol book that instructed what

images are to be taken for specific exams and then it was

lunchtime. Jody and I went to the cafeteria together. The

place was packed with interns and residents drinking coffee

and comparing stories about what they had seen today. You

could tell who the attending physicians were because they

were more serious, usually alone and walking with purpose.

There were a variety of other people rushing in and out in

hopes of grabbing a little bit of food before getting back to

where ever they needed to be. The place was buzzing. We

sat and ate with the anticipation of what the rest of the day

would entail.

After lunch we returned to the department and

found Joe for instruction. We were going to start shooting

rays. He put us in the chest room. That was one of the

easiest x-rays to take and that was what we were going to

do for the rest of the afternoon. Until we have a license we

have to be with a registered technologist and that would be

Joe for now. He handed me the first order and told me to go

and get the patient. I did and led the gentleman into the

room. I double checked his name and date of birth and

confirmed that he was there for a chest x-ray. I then asked

him to take off his shirt and lay it on the chair. Joe and Jody

were in the room and then Joe showed us how to adjust the

bucky to the correct position and how to line up the patient

properly so as to get all of the anatomy on the image. The

goal is to not repeat any images if possible. We took the

first image and then positioned the patient for the second

view from the side, called a lateral view. We gave the

breathing instructions and took the picture. Then we went

to check the images before we let the patient go just in case

we needed to repeat anything. The images looked good and

the patient left. The next patient was Jody's and the process

began again. After four or five patients Joe started hanging

back and letting us take the shots. The repetition was good

and I felt more comfortable each time. This was just the

beginning I thought to myself. We need to learn every view

for every part of the body, and then learn the vessels in

order to work in special procedures and the cath lab. I was

excited though and couldn't wait to be fully trained and out

of school. This is a great job.

It was three o'clock and we only had thirty minutes

left in our shift for today. The second shift crew was

coming in and relieving the day shift. Jody and I were

going to get at least one more patient done before leaving. I

went out to get the next patient and I saw Alex walking

down the hall with two other technologists. I stopped in my

tracks and looked down, not sure if he would recognize me

from the bar. They walked by talking and I was

disappointed that he gave no indication that I was even

standing there let alone recognize me. I looked up and

called for my patient. I went back over to the chest room

and Jody was in there to help me. My eyes glanced over to

the window that the technologist stands behind when

making an exposure and saw Alex and the two other men

he was with standing there. I looked away and kept talking

to my patient. I felt awkward all of the sudden and my

earlier confidence faded. Why were they standing there

staring at us? I got the patient positioned and walked out

with Jody to make the exposure. I gave the breathing

instructions and we took the picture. They just stood there

watching us. Where did Joe go? I went into the room and

positioned the patient for the second picture. We took the

shot and there they stood. I went in and instructed the

patient to have a seat and that I was going to check the

images before they left. I walked out and I saw Jody talking

to the three of them. As I came around to the exposure area

Jody said, "Isabella, this is Alex, Terry and Mathew. Joe had to leave a little early so he asked Terry to observe us for this last exam."

I smiled and said hi and kept moving toward the viewing area to check my films. Terry walked up behind me to check them as well and the other two stayed behind.

"They look good. You can push these through and let the patient go." Terry instructed.

I nodded and said, "Okay, thanks."

"How was your first day?"

"It was good. I learned a lot already."

Terry was a large, muscular African American man with a diamond stud earing in one ear. He wore his scrubs a little snug like Alex did so you could see the mass of muscles in

his arms. My guess was that he was in his early twenties. I

glanced at his badge. He was staff and not a student.

"How long have you worked here?" I asked him.

"It will be three years in December."

"Do you like it?"

"Yeah, I work the second shift and I do diagnostic

and CT. There is a lot of trauma, which is what I like. You

should do a second shift rotation once you hit the second

semester. It's where all the cool people work anyway." He

winked when he said that and laughed.

I followed him back to the chest room and let my

patient go. Alex and Mathew were talking and laughing and

barely glanced at me when I walked by. Poor Jody was just standing there as they ignored her.

"Thanks for your help Terry." I said before we left.

"My pleasure ladies. Are you back tomorrow?"

"Yeah, we are here Wednesday's and Thursday's."

"See you then. Have a good night." Terry said and smiled. He seemed like a nice guy.

Before I walked away with Jody I said, "Nice to meet you guys," and kept walking after I said it. They paused from talking and looked at me.

I heard Mathew say, "Nice meeting you too." I didn't hear Alex say anything. I wasn't sure I liked him very much.

We left totally jazzed about our day. We decided to celebrate and go to Patty's for a burger. The place was dead on a Wednesday and we sat at the bar and ate and talked to the bartender, Pete. He was an older guy who looked like a biker. He had long grey hair that was tied back in a ponytail, tattoos and a chain going from his wallet to his belt loop. I never understood that look. We were talking his ear off and I am sure he didn't care but he listened politely and nodded at the appropriate times.

"You girls sure look different in your hospital 'get up' and hair pulled back."

I laughed. I guess we would look a lot different outside of our t-shirts and short skirts.

"Hey Pete, did you know that Alex works over at the hospital too?" I don't know why I brought this up. Who cares, right? I just can't figure him out.

He just looked at me for a long moment. "You got a thing for that boy young lady?"

I was stunned that he said that to me. Why would he think that? Jody laughed when he said it and I wondered what was so funny. "No, I was just surprised to see him there that's all."

Pete never did answer me and went to wait on a customer at the other end of the bar. Jody and I paid and left when we were done.

By the time Friday rolled around I was exhausted

and enjoyed sleeping in. I hadn't been back to Tim's since

Tuesday and I was sure that he would want to rendezvous

this weekend. I laid around in front of the TV and then did

some homework. Tonight Tony was coming into the bar to

have his good-bye dinner with me. I smiled at the thought

of seeing him and then became sad knowing that it would

be the last time. Tears stung my eyes at the reality of this. I

showered and packed a bag just in case Tim invited me

over and then I left for work. I told my mom before I left

that I was staying at Jody's, certain Tim would call.

It was busy and my section was non-stop. It should

prove to be a good tip night. At nine Tony came in as

promised. I saw him and waved. He waited for me to come over to him and tell him where to sit. I motioned for Jody to come over.

"Tony, this is my friend Jody. Jody, this is Tony."

"Hi, it's nice to meet you." Jody said as she exchanged a handshake with him.

"It's nice to meet you too."

"I am going to take my break now if it is okay with you." I said to her.

"Yeah, I will cover your section."

Most of the people in my section were gone and we had a little lull before the next wave of people came in. I slid into the booth across from Tony and smiled. "So this is it. Are you ready for the big move?"

He smiled back at me and reached over to take my hand. "I am ready, but I will miss you."

I sat holding his hand and looked at him. "I will miss you too. You are going to find everything you are looking for up there."

"Will I? I am starting to think that what I was looking for was right here all along."

I was trying to comprehend just what he was saying to me. Is this what Kate meant by I wasn't seeing him? Did he hope that our relationship was more? I didn't even have time to say anything when Tim, Mike, Tammy, Yvette and

Greg walked in. They made a loud entrance as they talked

and laughed and then went silent when I was spotted sitting

in a booth holding Tony's hand obviously talking about

something serious. I saw them and pulled my hand away. I

saw Tim walking up to the table. I was scared. I knew how

this looked.

"What are you doing?" Tim said with venom in his

voice.

"I was talking with Tony and we were going to have

dinner since he leaves for Seattle tomorrow." I said trying

to explain.

"That's not how it looks. Is this what you are doing

every Friday night?" Tim shot out.

"Tim, don't be rude. You know that Tony and I are friends."

"Oh yeah, I can see that. What else is he Isabella?"

"What is that supposed to mean?" I was angry now.

Tony then started to slide out of the seat. "I should go. Bye Isabella."

"No, don't go. You don't have to go. We were supposed to have dinner."

"Oh don't let me ruin your date. You two go right ahead, I won't get in your way." Tim indignantly sneered.

Tony had already slid out of the seat and was walking toward the door.

"Tim, shut up. I wasn't doing anything wrong!"

"Don't you tell me to shut up. Who do you think you are? I am not the one cheating."

"I am not cheating. I am taking my break and having dinner with my friend. That is all."

"Well that's not how it looked when I walked in here. "

Before I could say anything more Michelle grabbed my arm. "Can I see you in the back?" I followed her to the back room behind the bar. "What is going on? Is that your boyfriend?"

"Yes."

"You two can not get into a lovers quarrel in the middle of the bar! Do you got it?"

"Yes. I am sorry, I didn't mean for, I mean…"

"Stop. I don't know or care what is going on but this ends now. Pick it up at home. Got it?"

"Yes."

"Your break is over. Get back to work."

When I returned they were all gone. Jody came up to me and gave me a hug. "I am sorry."

"Me too. How embarrassing. I can't believe he acted like that."

"Did he know that Tony was coming in to have dinner with you?"

"No. I didn't think it was a big deal."

"I know, and it isn't, but imagine how he felt when he walked in and saw you holding Tony's hand."

As she said it I felt like a heal. I didn't consider how Tim must have felt. Now what was I going to do? Tammy didn't even try to help me. She knows that I am only friends with Tony. Why didn't she help me? How am I going to get him to believe me? The night dragged on after that and I just went through the motions. Alex and his gang came in at midnight like they do every Friday night and as always Michelle took care of them. I noticed that Terry was always with him but never Mathew. I wondered why. I guess they just weren't as good of friends. I decided to send Tim a text.

Please don't be mad at me. I was just having dinner with a friend nothing more. Please believe me. I miss you.

Isa

A half an hour went by and he hadn't responded. I decided to try Tammy.

Are you there? Is Tim with you? He won't respond to my text.

Isa

Tammy did respond which was the least she could do after being silent and not defending me.

He's not with us. We went to the APP and he left. Didn't say where he was going.

T

Where would he go? Maybe he went home? After my shift I will drive over there. I can't leave things like this. Jody came up to me while I was standing there thinking about my plan for after work.

"Are you okay? Do you want to stay at my house tonight?"

"No, I am going to swing by Tim's and try to make this right."

"Are you sure you don't want to wait until morning? Let things cool off a little bit?"

"I can't. I have to make him see that it was nothing."

She smiled empathetically and stood there with me.

We watched Alex's group shoot pool from a far. I

wondered who these people were that he hung out with on

the weekend. I didn't recognize any of them from school.

The night finally came to an end and I went to my

car and headed for Tim's. When I got there the house was

dark. I wondered if he was in there asleep or not home at

all. It was almost two thirty in the morning and the bars

were all closed by now. I pulled into the driveway and only

saw Greg's car there. Where was Tim's car? I sat in the car

and sent another text.

I am at your house. Can I come in?

Isa

I sat there about ten minutes and then called his cell. It went to voicemail. "Tim, I am so sorry that I hurt you. That was not my intention, but please understand that I didn't do anything wrong. I know how it must have looked and I am sorry. Please just talk to me."

I pulled out of the driveway and drove home. When I got there I fell into bed feeling miserable. I would go by again tomorrow and try to talk to him.

When I woke up I felt like I had been out all night and hadn't slept. I grabbed my phone and looked at it. No messages. Why was he being so stubborn? I decided to send a text to Tony to apologize for the scene last night and to wish him a safe trip.

Have a safe trip. I am sorry about last night.

Isabella

Bella,

I am sorry too. You know where to find me if you

should ever need anything.

Tony

Somehow I couldn't help but to feel like that was

the last time we were going to speak. My heart felt like it

was shattering into a thousand pieces. I got up and

showered and left for Tim's house. When I got there his car

was in the driveway. He must have today off. I got out and

went to the door and rang the doorbell. He opened the door

and just stared at me. He was unshowered and unshaven.

He didn't look like he had slept much last night.

"Can I come in?"

"Why?'

"To talk this out with you, that's why." There was

desperation in my voice.

"What's to talk about?"

"Would you let me explain? What you saw

yesterday was totally innocent. He took my hand when he

was saying good-bye, that's all, really. Please believe me."

"Why should I believe you?"

"Why shouldn't you?" I was raising my voice. "What have I ever done to make you not trust me?"

"Well how about me walking into a bar with all of our friends only to see you embraced with another man? How about that!"

"I wasn't embraced! He took my hand for a minute, that's all! You act like you caught us in bed together or something! This is ridiculous. Ask Tammy, she knows that we are just friends. Ask her."

"No, I am not going to ask her anything. I saw what I saw."

"So what are you saying? Are you saying that we are through?"

He just stared at me saying nothing. So much for 'I am in love with you'. I decided to bring that up. "I thought that you loved me. That's what you said."

"That is before I knew this side of you."

"What side of me? The side that has friends?"

"How dumb can you be Isabella? You can't tell when someone wants to get into your pants? Really?"

"What are you talking about? Nobody has been in my pants but you and you know it." I am really mad now.

"So you say. How many were there before me, huh? You play the innocent young thing very well."

"I am leaving. If that is what you think of me then fine. We have nothing more to talk about." I turned and walked back to my car. He didn't come after me. He just

quietly closed the door. I drove off and stopped at Patty's

for lack of a better place to go. I sat in the parking lot and

cried. I didn't want to go home where my parents would

question what was wrong, Tammy is with Mike and I

didn't want to bother Jody. I don't know how long I was

there when someone knocked on my window. I jumped a

foot off of the seat startled. I looked out the window and

saw Alex. What was he doing here on a Saturday morning?

I rolled down the window and looked at him with a blotchy

red face and puffy eyes.

     "You okay in there?"

     I nodded. "Yes, I am fine."

He stared at me with those serious big brown eyes.

He had on a white t-shirt that, like Terry's, hugged his

massive arms, and faded denim jeans. He had a thick gold

chain on that I hadn't noticed in the past. He truly was a

beautiful creature to look at. "You don't look fine Isabella."

How did he know my name? The man has never

said more than two words to me and ignores me every time

I see him. I didn't know what to say as I sat there staring

back at him. "What are you doing here?"

"Picking up a car from last night that one of my

impaired friends couldn't drive for themselves. What are

you doing here?"

How was I going to answer that? Well, I am here crying my eyes out because my boyfriend dumped me and I have no friends to turn to so I am in the bar parking lot alone.

When I didn't answer he said, "Come on, let's get a cup of coffee until you are feeling better." He opened the door and waited for me to get out. I did not argue with him and got out. He motioned me to a navy blue Nissan GT-R. He opened the door for me and I got in. This was a beautiful car. I wonder who it belongs to in that mysterious group that he hangs around with?

"Where's your truck?"

"Terry dropped me off and he is taking my truck back to my place."

"This is a nice car. Who does it belong to?"

"Oscar."

That meant nothing to me and he knew it. We just went around the corner to a Starbucks and we got out. We went in and he ordered a venti coffee black. He looked at me so I could order what I wanted. I got a caramel macchiato. He paid and I thanked him. We found a quiet place to sit in the back corner of the coffee shop. We sat and he looked at me. He definitely is a man of few words.

"How do you like working at Patty's?"

"It's fine. It gives me some money while I am in school."

He nodded slightly and he continued to stare at me. We sat quiet for a while and the silent company was actually nice. It wasn't long before I felt that I needed to explain why I was in the parking lot crying. "I, uh, my boyfriend, well, last night at Patty's I was having dinner with a friend of mine and my boyfriend came in and saw us. He didn't like it even though I explained that we were just friends. He broke things off with me because of it." I glanced up at Alex feeling like an idiot. "I tried to go by this morning to explain but he wasn't interested. I didn't have any place else to go so I drove to the bar to be alone

for awhile."

He nodded again and said nothing. I twirled my

coffee cup in a circle feeling like a complete jerk.

"Why don't you have any place to go?"

"I don't want my parents to see me upset. They

really didn't even know that I was seeing him so they

wouldn't understand what is going on. My best friend has a

boyfriend that she is attached to by the hip, and Jody and I

just met so I didn't want to burden her."

"Do you live at home with your parents?"

"Yes."

"Why don't they know who your boyfriend is?"

That's a good question. Why haven't I ever brought Tim to my house to meet my parents? "We haven't been dating very long and the right time never came up for him to meet them." We sat again in silence for a while. "How about you? How long have you been with your girlfriend?"

He looked at me for a long moment. "How do you know that I have a girlfriend?"

My face blushed. "I saw you with her at the college."

"Five years."

Wow, that's a long time. They must have been together in high school too.

"You look like you are feeling better. Should we go back to your car?"

"Okay, sure. Thank you for the coffee. That was nice of you."

"You're welcome."

We went back out to the GT-R and drove back to my crappy 1968 Mustang that wasn't fully restored. I thanked Alex again and got back into my car. He drove off after I started my car. I made my way home reviewing the events of today in my head.

Chapter 15

Several weeks went by and I heard nothing from

Tim. I felt sad every day but immersed myself in school

and work. I was able to pick up some Saturday day shifts at

Patty's for extra money, which I really needed. I would see

Alex, Terry and Mathew on my clinical days, but not much

had changed other then some small talk. Alex seemed to

just watch me from a far, like he was making sure that I

was okay after finding me in a parking lot decompensating.

I heard that he was leaving for Cancun for a week with his Barbie doll girlfriend, Susana. School was going well and Jody and I were able to do a lot of the exams at Arizona General independently and have a Radiographer check them before letting the patients go.

Halloween was around the corner and it seemed like there were parties everywhere this year. Tammy says that Tim is miserable without me. I wish I could believe her. She invited me to a Halloween party this weekend at her and Mikes new house. They are renting near the airport since they both work there. I am scared to go, but she calls me everyday to make sure that I will be there.

I dressed up as a pirate as I got ready to go to the

Halloween party. It was the easiest costume that I could

find on short notice. I got there early to help Tammy set up

and to my surprise Tim was there too. He was dressed up

like a cop. I said hello as I walked by, and followed Tammy

around to receive instructions. Tim smiled and said hi but

he wasn't exactly warm and fuzzy.

The night progressed and people started to show. I

knew most of the people here since they are mostly from

the airlines. I sat there with a beer in my hand just

watching the people around me. I noticed Brenda was here

and couldn't help but to notice that she was alone. I wonder

where Martin is? Maybe he is working. She was also

hanging on Tim. That's weird; I have never seen her act like that before. Greg and Yvette were here too. I heard that they bought a house together and moved out of Tim's place. Kelly and Tom came up to me and gave me a hug. They were dressed up like M & M's.

"How are you?" Kelly asks me enthusiastically.

"I am good. How are you guys?"

"The same as always. Miss seeing you at work though."

"Me too."

"How's school?"

"It is good. The clinical's are the best part. I can't wait until I get paid for what I am doing though."

"That's great. I am glad to hear that things are going well for you. Have you heard from Tony since he moved?"

I think my eyes welled up with tears at the thought of how we said good-bye. "No, I haven't heard from him, have you?"

"No, we weren't that close."

I nodded and didn't say anything more. Kelly and Tom went to look for Tammy to see if she would give them a tour of the house and I sat alone again. After about a half hour I decided to go. I was bored out of my mind. I was surprised at how much I had changed over the last couple of months. I didn't have that much in common with these people any more. I walked out to my car and heard someone behind me. I walked a little faster and the

footsteps behind me picked up the pace as well. I finally

reached my car and I was frantically trying to open it when

two hands land on the car trapping me between the arms

they were attached to. I spun around and saw it was Tim.

"What the hell are you doing scaring me like that!"

"I am sorry. I just wanted to stop you from getting

away."

Obviously he had been drinking. "Do you need a

ride home Tim or are you staying here with Tammy and

Mike?"

He looked at me for a minute and then smiled. "I

need a ride."

"Okay, get in, and don't barf in my car."

"I am not going to barf." He said annoyed.

I started driving and he told me to go west on Valencia. "Tim you don't live that way."

"Just go that way. Please."

I turned as he requested and kept driving. "Now where?"

"Turn right on Camino de Oeste."

I turned as directed. It was a residential neighborhood. I drove slow not knowing where we were going.

"Pull in here." He pointed to a house on the right at the end of the cul-de-sac.

I pulled into the driveway and sat there. "Where are we Tim? Who lives here?"

"I put in a bid on this house."

My mouth dropped open. "Wow, that's a big step. Congratulations, it is really nice."

"I find out next week if I get it."

I didn't say anything else. I just sat and listened.

"If I get it would you consider living here with me?"

"What? Tim, I am not sure if you remember but you basically told me that you didn't trust me and then broke up with me. You wouldn't talk to me. Why would you want me to live with you and why do you think I would after all

of that?"

"Because. Because I really do love you and I think

you love me too. I miss you. I miss being with you and I

want us to start a life together."

I just sat there dumb founded. I didn't see this

coming at all. Did Tammy know about this house? Did she

know that he wanted me to live here with him? Is that why

she was adamant that I go to the party? "Tim, you broke

my heart. I can't just move in with you. It is going to take

time to heal and rebuild this if we can."

"Please just say that you will think about it."

"Tim, I can't afford to live here with you even if I wanted to. I only work one, sometimes two days a week. I am in school and I just can't do it."

"You don't need to rent from me Isabella. It is my house. I am inviting you to stay in it with me. I am not asking you for any money. Just say you will think about it."

Why does he say things that make me want to be with him? Is it that I just want to be wanted and needed? What would I say to my parents? They haven't even met him. "I will think about it." I heard myself say.

"Will you come home with me tonight?"

"Tim, I don't know. I should just drop you off at your house. If you need a ride back to your car in the morning then I will come pick you up and drive you to get

it."

"Isabella, please let me hold you. Please."

I didn't commit to anything. I backed out of the

driveway and headed to his townhouse. We didn't speak for

the entire ride. My parents weren't expecting me home. I

could stay without detection but did I want to? I pulled up

in front of his place and killed the engine. "If I stay I am

leaving early in the morning because I have a lot of

homework to get done. Deal?"

He nodded and got out of the car. I followed him up

to the door and we went inside. The familiar surroundings

made me sad that I had been away for so long. We walked

to his room and he opened his dresser drawer and handed

me a t-shirt to change into. I took it and went into the

bathroom to wash my face and change. I came out and

crawled into bed. Tim went next to change and wash up.

He came out and crawled in next to me. We snuggled up

together and fell asleep. The warmth of him wrapped

around me was comforting and I slept soundly enjoying his

embrace.

　　　When morning came I awoke early. Tim was still

wrapped around me sleeping. I slipped out, gathered my

things and left. I am sure that Mike and Tammy could bring

his car back to him. I drove home and showered and started

my homework. I was distracted all day about his proposal.

Move in with him? Just like that? Maybe he really did miss

me and sees that now?

Later in the day I received a text message from

Tammy.

So did you guys kiss and make up?

Tam

Kiss, no. As far as making up, that is still on the

table.

Isa

Seriously Isabella? You are going to make him wait

to see if you will get back with him? Hasn't he suffered

enough?

Hasn't he suffered enough? Is she being serious? I

went silent not wanting to answer her.

Chapter 16

The next week went by as usual. Saturday morning

Tim called my phone. "Good morning sunshine." He said

in a soft mischievous voice.

"Good morning."

"I closed on the house yesterday".

"That's great Tim! Congratulations."

"Do you want to come and see it?"

"I would love to. What time should I meet you

there?"

"I will be there all day today cleaning and painting. I will probably get a lot of my stuff moved in too since I really don't have that much. Most of the stuff that was in the townhouse was Greg's and he took it with him.

"Okay, I am going to get some homework done this morning and then I will come by. Let's say noon? I will bring lunch to celebrate. How does Chinese sound?"

"Sounds great." He paused for a minute and then said, "Isabella. I really do miss you."

I smiled on the other end of the phone. "Miss you too. I will see you for lunch." I hung up and dove into my homework. I wanted to get it all done before I left." The morning was gone before I knew it and I showered up and headed for Chinese on my way to Tim's. I hoped that I

remembered which house it was since it was dark when I

saw it last weekend.

When I turned onto his street I saw his car in the

driveway and knew I was in the right place. I pulled up

next to him since the driveway was big enough for two cars

to park side by side. The outside of the house was beige

stucco. There were two arches in the front of the house

giving it an old Spanish feel to it. It was pretty and I liked

the feel of it already. I grabbed the food bag and walked up

to the door. Tim answered and smiled.

"Hi." He said as he leaned over and kissed me

gently. "Come in." He moved to the side and I stepped in.

It was very quaint. Saltillo tile with ceramic talavera inlays covered the floor. The living room was to the right and was sunken lower then the foyer entryway. Straight ahead was a family room and I followed Tim in that direction. The family room has sliding glass doors leading to the back yard. I glanced out as I walked by on our way to the kitchen. It was small but it had a pool. The kitchen was right off the family room. It had dark cabinets and tiled countertops. I set the food on the counter. "It's beautiful Tim. You did a good job finding this place."

He smiled and took my hand. "Let me show you the rest." We walked back through the family room and then turned right down a hallway. There was a bathroom on the left, and a laundry closet across the hall from it. A little bit further down the hall was a bedroom on the left that had nothing in it but a desk and chair. Across from that was his bedroom. It was considered the master bedroom since it had a bathroom attached to it and was the bigger of the two bedrooms. He had already moved his furniture in. The bathroom had an oval garden tub, a separate shower with glass surrounding it and a double sink vanity. The tile on the counter matched the kitchen counters.

"Do you like it?"

"Oh yes, it is very nice."

"I am glad." He stood behind me with his arms wrapped around my waist. "The offer still stands you know."

I nodded in acknowledgement saying nothing. He kissed my neck and I felt goose bumps on my arms. He felt my reaction and decided to keep going. He nuzzled my neck some more and slid his hands down over my hips and back up to my waist. I closed my eyes enjoying his gentle touch. He was still behind me and slid his hands under my shirt. His hands slid over my belly and then slowly up to my breasts. He caressed me and I leaned my head back onto his shoulder. My breathing was getting harder as he reached behind me and unclipped my bra. As it sprung free his other hand came up and rubbed over my nipple. They

became hard and taught immediately. His other hand came

back around and unbuttoned my jeans. His had dove into

my pants and found my wetness. I wanted this and my

arousal was clear. I felt his erection pressing behind me and

I pressed my butt back against him and moved with the

rhythm of his caressing. His whispered in my ear, "I missed

you."

"I missed you too." I could barely get the words out

already ready to orgasm from his touch. He felt my urgency

rising and plunged two fingers into me. I gasped and his

swift movement took me over the edge, I yelled out and

arched backwards, my head on his shoulder. He didn't stop

as I came. He kept his movements going and I screamed in

delight and thought that my legs would give out, but he was

holding me with his other arm. I opened my eyes and

realized he was watching us in the bathroom mirror. I

smiled slightly a little embarrassed at seeing myself like

that. He pushed my pants down and moved us forward

toward the sink. He reached behind me and undid his pants

and pulled them down. He bent me forward and I became

nervous not knowing what to expect. I grabbed the counter

and I felt his hand behind me. He felt forward and rubbed

me again and then I felt him penetrate into me. There was a

lot more pressure in this position but it felt good. I looked

down not wanting to see myself in the mirror. He grabbed

my hips and began moving me back and forth. Slowly at

first and then gradually picking up the pace. I could feel

myself building again and my breathing was a give away. I

groaned knowing that it was coming, I was going to come

again already. I heard him say, "Oh yeah baby, give it to

me. Give it to me hard." He started moving too, slamming

into me hard repeatedly. I yelled out each time until I

couldn't take it anymore I started to orgasm and tried to

arch up but his hand went to the back of my head holding me

forward. I yelled as I came, I think harder than I have

before. He came too and I could feel him explode in me. I

leaned over the counter trying to slow my breathing. He

pulled out of me and rested his head on my back. I could

feel semen running down my leg and I didn't care, I was too tired to move. "Thank you." Tim said with his head still resting on my back. I smiled and nodded still unable to speak. "We could do this all of the time if you were here with me." I smiled again and nodded. "Does that mean that you will stay here with me?"

"Yes."

I felt him give me light kisses up my back. "Really? You will stay?"

"I will stay."

He smiled. "Let's eat."

I laughed and stood up. As I turned around a towel hit me in the face that he had thrown. "Thanks for that." I laughed as I took it and cleaned myself up.

We ate Chinese on the floor because he didn't have a kitchen table yet. When we were done, we went to the hardware store and bought paint and supplies. Before I knew it the day was done. "I should get going."

"I thought you were going to move in with me?"

"Well not this minute. I don't have my things here with me."

"I will go with you to get your things."

"Tim, I have to tell my parents. They haven't even met you yet."

"So I will go meet them and then we will bring your things back here."

"Tim, my parents aren't going to like this. I should talk to them by myself first."

"They will talk you out of it Isabella. I need you. I need you here with me."

I walked up and put my hand on his cheek. "It will be fine, trust me." I couldn't help but to notice the desperation on his face. He really wanted this.

"When? When will you be back?"

"Tomorrow. I will bring my things tomorrow."

"Do you promise?"

"Yes."

He nodded in agreement and we walked to my car. He kissed me deeply before I got in to leave. I could feel his longing and I was glad. I was glad that he missed me and needed me.

While I was driving I called Jody.

"Hey, it's me. You got a minute?"

"Yeah, what's up?"

"I agreed to move in with Tim."

She was silent for a minute. "Isabella, are you sure about this? It was only a few weeks ago that your heart was broken in two by him."

"I know, I know, but I can tell that he learned from that. He really misses me and wants me."

"How are you going to tell your parents?"

"I don't know. I am freaking out about that part. I told Tim that I would move my stuff tomorrow."

"Tomorrow! Well, good luck with that." She said with sarcasm. After a moment of silence she said, "Call me if you need my help and let me know how it goes telling your parents. They are not going to dig this decision."

"I know. I am scared."

"You should be."

"Thanks for that. I was calling for encouragement."

"Oh, okay, well I am sure it will all be fine. How was that?"

I laughed. "You suck. I will call you later."

She laughed too, "Good luck."

Chapter 17

When I got home I just sat in my car for several minutes trying to get up my nerve to go in and talk to my folks. They are nice, calm people, but they are going to be disappointed in me and I couldn't bear that. I got out and went in to face the music and start packing my things. I went to my room first. I looked around it and felt sad. I didn't have any great need to leave. I pulled out two suitcases. I wouldn't need to bring any furniture since technically it belonged to my parents and not me anyway. I put clothes in the suitcases. I could come back during the week for the rest. I went to the bathroom and packed up my toiletries. I found my pack of birth control pills hidden

behind the extra hairspray and shampoo bottles. Oh God. I

stopped taking these after I didn't hear from Tim for a

couple of weeks. I figured that since I wasn't seeing anyone

anymore that I would just stop. I hadn't anticipated a

reunion. I opened the packet and popped a pill into my

mouth. The chances of me ovulating right now are slim. I

am sure it will be okay. I finished packing up and went out

to talk to my mom. I sat down at the kitchen table quietly.

She was cooking dinner and turned to look me and smiled.

"Well hello there stranger. Will you be here for

dinner?"

"Yep."

"Good. That will be nice. I know how busy you have been."

Well, here goes. "Mom. I have to talk to you about something."

She turned slowly to look at me. Her smile had faded. She turned off the burners on the stove and came over to the table with concern on her face. She sat in the chair across from me. "What is it?" She asked softly, sensing something was wrong.

"Mom, I met someone. Someone I really care a lot about."

She smiled. "Oh thank God. You scared me."

"Mom, I have decided to move in with him."

The smile was gone again and the look of pain and shock spread across her face. "What? How long have you known him? Why haven't you brought him here to meet us? I really don't think living with someone before marriage is a good idea Isabella. It's not appropriate, it's not how you were raised."

Well, there it was, here comes the disappointment. "His name is Tim and we have been dating since June." I left out the recent separation. "I didn't bring him here because I wanted to be sure this was someone worth bringing home first. He just bought a house and invited me to live in it with him."

"You can't afford it." My mom shot out matter a factly.

"He isn't asking any rent from me mom."

"I bet he isn't."

Whoa, where did that come from? "Mom, please trust me. Please trust that you raised me to be a good person. You were married already by the time you were my age."

"Yes Isabella, married, not living in sin!"

I lowered my eyes to the table. I felt so ashamed. I knew what this would do to them. What was my dad going to say if mom was acting like this?

"There is nothing that I am going to be able to say to change your mind is there?"

I shook my head no. She sighed loudly.

"When were you planning on moving?"

"Tomorrow."

"Tomorrow!"

"It's not like I have a lot to move mom. I only have my clothes."

We sat in silence at that point. She then got up and continued to make dinner. I got up and went back to my room. That was every bit as bad as I thought it would be. Maybe I won't stay for dinner. Maybe I will just go to

Tim's tonight. I laid down on my bed and closed my eyes.

An hour later I heard a knock on my door.

"Come in." I said.

The door opened and my dad walked in. He closed the door behind him. I have been dreading this conversation ever since I talked to mom earlier. He sat down on the edge of my bed.

"Your mom tells me that you are moving out."

I nodded.

"Are you sure about this boy Isabella? This seems very sudden. You have a bright future ahead of you. We just don't want to see you do something that will hurt you or your future."

"I know dad. I think this is a good decision for me, I really do. Please just trust me."

He leaned over and kissed my forehead. "I don't like letting my little girl go, but you are an adult now. You need to make your own decisions. Just remember that you can always come home if you want to."

I nodded my head letting him know that I understood.

"And I hope that you will at least introduce us to this young man."

"I will dad, I promise."

"Okay then, lets go have dinner. Your mother is waiting for us."

I smiled and walked out to the kitchen with him.

After dinner I sent Tim a text.

Can you come meet my folks tomorrow? It would mean a lot to them.

Isa

Yeah, I work in the morning but can come by after.

T

Thanks.

The next morning I woke up and packed some more. I went and got boxes the night before so I could bring everything I wanted to in one trip. At about five Tim pulled up in front of the house. I met him outside.

"How did it go telling them that you were moving in with me?"

"Hard but I got through it. It probably would have gone better if they had met you before we decided to live together."

"You're probably right, but I am here now." He gave me a kiss and smiled down at me. He looked happy.

We walked up to the house and went inside. My mom heard us and came out of the kitchen.

"Mom, this is Tim. Tim, this is my mom Cheryl."

He extended his hand. "It's nice to meet you."

"It's nice to meet you too." She said politely as she shook his hand back.

My dad came out from the family room. "And this is my dad, Richard. Dad this is Tim."

"It's nice to meet you. You take good care of my little girl, do you hear me?"

Tim grinned at him. "Yes sir I will. I promise."

We stood there with uncomfortable silence. "Okay, well you kids run along now. Did you leave your address for your mother?" Dad said looking at me.

"Yes dad. It's on the counter." I gave my mom and dad a kiss on the cheek. "I will call lots, I promise." I led Tim to my room to start carrying my things out to our cars. My mom looked teary eyed but went back to the kitchen to finish dinner.

Before we left I went inside one more time to say good-bye to my parents. I was off on a new adventure and I felt happy and excited. I came back out and got in my car. Tim was waiting for me so we could follow each other back to the house.

We got everything unloaded and we were both tired. I had class tomorrow and was ready to go crash. Tim wrapped his arms around me. "Ready to turn in for the

night?" I shook my head in agreement. He led me to the

bedroom and we crawled into bed. Of course Tim insisted

that we needed to consummate our new relationship in this

house and we didn't really sleep until some time later.

Chapter 18

When I got to class Jody was already there waiting

for me. "How did it go with your parental units?"

I sighed loudly. "It was really hard. I felt so guilty,

but I moved into Tim's last night."

"Congratulations."

I laughed and then class started. I saw Alex as we

were walking to our second class. I smiled and gave a small

wave trying to not be detected by anyone. He grinned like

he always does and gave me a nod. Alex and I had become

friends over the past few weeks. Well, I think we are

friends. It is always hard to tell with Alex. You never know

what he is thinking. I always look forward to seeing him

though. Something about him makes me feel safe and

protected, and turned on but I choose to ignore that.

Especially since he is very taken and I am back with Tim. I

wonder where the girlfriend is today? She is usually

hanging on him.

On Wednesday at the hospital, I saw Terry and

Mathew coming onto their shift as I ended mine, but no

sign of Alex. That was strange since they were always

together. I stopped and made small talk with them, then

made my way to get my lunch bag and wait for Jody to come out of the OR. Alex was in the lunchroom alone pouring a cup of coffee. I walked in behind him. "Hey Alex. How's it going?"

He looked sideways at me and said, "Fine." His tone was clipped and I could tell something wasn't right.

I walked up next to him and looked at him. I put a hand on his arm, which sent excitement through me, and I let go as fast I touched him. "You okay?"

He looked at me but his eyes were dark. Dark and scary. There was anger in there. I have never seen that look before. "I am fine Isa."

I nodded in agreement. Clearly he didn't want to talk but I knew something was not right. "Okay, well, I am here if you ever need anything, or an ear to unload into."

A sideways grin appeared and he said nothing. I turned and walked out of the break room. Jody was on her way down the hall. "Sorry, I got relieved late." She said.

"It's fine, don't rush." She grabbed her stuff out of her locker and we left.

"Something is wrong with Alex." I blurted out in the car.

Jody laughed. "How can you tell? He doesn't talk."

"Very funny. He talks. He is actually very sweet when you get to know him."

She looked at me and I kept my eyes on the road. "That had the sound of more than friends."

"No we are friends. He has a super hot model girlfriend and I have Tim."

Jody continued to look at me. "Then why does your face light up when you see him?"

"It doesn't."

"Isabella, don't get mad, but I see your face, you don't. You glow when you see that man."

"Nope."

"Okay, whatever you say."

"Are we going to the Tech Dinner?" I asked changing the subject. The Tech Dinner was a dinner sponsored by the Radiologist's at the hospital. It is to celebrate National Rad Tech week, which is the second week in November. Only the techs and students are invited. No spouses or significant others are allowed.

"Free food and booze, I am in." Jody declared.

We laughed together. "I was hoping you would say that because I wanted to go too."

Chapter 19

Friday was another full house at Patty's. I had

regulars now and could pull down decent tips. Alex and his

posse came in as usual. This time Alex wasn't shooting

pool. He was having a serious conversation with Terry.

Were they fighting? I watched from a far trying not to stare.

Something was wrong. I saw Michelle deliver two rounds

of shots in less than thirty minutes. That was unusual for

Alex. I have never seen him do shots. He drinks beer but

never loses control.

By the end of the night Alex was definitely drunk.

Terry was paying the tab and their friends had all left. Alex

was slumped in a chair just staring straight ahead. I went

over and pulled up a chair since we were closed now and

just cleaning up. "Hey my friend. What's going on?"

He turned those dark eyes on me again. The same

ones I saw the other day at the hospital. He gave me a sad

smile and put his hand on my cheek. He still said nothing. I

swear I was ready to start panting with his hand on me. I

stared back. "What? Tell me what Alex?"

Before Alex could say anything, Terry walked up

and said, "Come on brother, let's get you home." He hauled

him out of the chair and put his arm over his shoulder in

order to help Alex walk. Alex went with him and never said a word.

"What was that all about?" Jody asked, "I have never seen Alex drunk."

"Me either." I said as I stared at the door they left through.

I didn't get home until almost three in the morning, which is the usual when I work Friday nights until close. The house was dark and I assumed that Tim was asleep. I made my way to the bedroom, but no Tim. I looked in the bathroom and then went back out to the living area and then to the kitchen. Tim wasn't home. How weird. I hope he is okay. I went to the message machine that was

flashing. There was a message from Union Air. Tim needed

to go in at seven in the morning tomorrow for a random

drug test. This is standard protocol for the airlines. They

randomly check all of their employees. I picked up my cell

phone and there were no messages. I sent him a text.

Where are you? Are you okay?

Isa

I decided to get ready for bed while I was waiting.

No response. I called his phone and there was no answer. I

was worried and sat up waiting. I dozed off about an hour

later and awoke when I heard Tim come in. He stumbled

into the bedroom and closed the door behind him a little too

hard.

I sat up and looked over at him confused at his loud

entrance. "Where were you? I was worried. Why didn't you

return my call?" I looked closer at him. He was trashed.

"Are you drunk?"

"Yeah" was all that he said and he crawled into bed

with his clothes on.

"Tim." I shook him. "Tim, you have to go in for a

drug test tomorrow, or today rather. There is a message

from work."

He was snoring already. What was this all about? Who was he with? Probably stupid Greg. I couldn't stand that guy. I set the alarm for 5:30 a.m. I will get him up so he makes it there on time.

The alarm went off and I tried to wake Tim up. "Come on you have to go in for your drug test. Tim, please get up. You are going to get in trouble if you don't show."

He rolled over. "I am not going."

"What do you mean? You have to go. It's mandatory that you show up."

"Everyone gets one miss. I will tell them that I didn't get the message, which I wouldn't have if you weren't here."

I stood there staring at him. Was he avoiding the

drug test or was he really just that tired? I couldn't sleep

now and left the house and went to Starbucks. I got my

usual and turned around to take a seat. Alex was sitting at

the corner table in the back staring out the window. I

walked up. "Mind if I join you?"

He turned his head and looked up me. His slow easy

grin appeared and he kicked the chair out.

"What are you doing here so early?" I asked

"I could ask you the same."

"I couldn't sleep. You were not in the best shape

last night, actually a few hours ago. I figured you would be

recovering all day."

"I am fine. It's nothing that coffee can't fix. Why can't you sleep?"

I didn't want to tell him the truth. He would think that I was a total flake, first for going back to Tim and second for not trusting him after all of that.

"It's nothing coffee can't fix." I replied.

He laughed and raised his cup to me.

"How was Cancun?" I asked.

His eyes darkened again. Oh boy, I guess something bad happened there.

"It was fine."

I nodded trying to think of a way to change the subject. "Are you going to the tech dinner?"

"Are you?'

"Yes, I am looking forward to it."

"Why?"

"Why what?"

"Why are you looking forward to it?"

"Free food and booze sounds like a fun night to me. I hear that everyone goes out dancing after the dinner every year. Should be fun don't you think?"

He nodded and grinned again. "Yeah, it sounds like fun."

"Are you patronizing me?"

He laughed out loud. "No."

"Yes you are you brat."

He laughed again, "No, I am not, really. Yes, I am going to go to the dinner."

"Good. You better sit with me and Jody okay."

"Okay, I will sit with you."

We finished our coffee and the sun was up.

"I should go home and get some homework done. You are very lucky to be done with all of this in December. Did the hospital sign you on?"

"Yes, I have a secured position."

"On second shift?"

"Yeah."

"Hey, how did you get here if Terry drove you home?"

"I took his car while he was sleeping."

I laughed and shook my head. "You boys are something else. See you next week."

I drove home. Tim was still in bed. His phone was buzzing. I picked it up and looked at it. It was from Brenda.

Did you get home okay?

He was with Brenda last night? That's weird, where was her husband and kids? I decided to answer.

He got home fine Brenda, thanks for asking.

No response. I was mad now. What the hell is going on? Why was he with her last night? I erased the message off of his phone and set it down. I then sent a text to

Tammy on my phone.

Was there a party last night?

Isa

What party? Not that I know of. Why?

T

Just wondering. Thanks.

Isa

I got out my homework and went to the kitchen to

work on it. Tim finally rolled out of bed at one o'clock in

the afternoon. "Good afternoon sunshine." I said without

looking up.

"What's that supposed to mean?" Tim said

defensive.

"Nothing. A little grumpy today are we? Where

were you last night?"

"Partying with Greg." He didn't even delay in his

answer.

"Could you at least call me or text me when you are

going to be out late so I don't worry?"

"Yeah, sure."

"You missed your drug test for work today."

"They will give me another date."

I shook my head in disbelief saying nothing. "I have

a dinner to go to the Thursday after next okay?"

"Okay, I will put it on my calendar."

"No need, it is only for the techs."

"You're not a tech yet."

"It's for the tech students too."

"So I can't go with you."

"No."

"I don't like it."

"I will be there with Jody. It's fine."

He looked mad but didn't say anything else.

Chapter 20

It was the night of the tech dinner and I went to Jody's after clinicals to get ready. I wore my Miss Me jeans that I loved and a Zebra print tank top. I chose some short heals and my black Chanel lipstick purse to accessorize my outfit. I pinned half my hair up in bobby pins and curled the rest to flow over my shoulders. Not bad I thought to myself. Jody looked fabulous in her jeans and solid t-shirt accessorized by a silk scarf. She also wore heals. We left following each other in our own cars just in case one of us wanted to leave early. We got to the restaurant about thirty

minutes late, which was fine since we didn't want to be the

first ones there. I immediately scanned the room and

spotted Alex and Terry sitting at the corner table. I hope

they saved us seats. "Come on, I see our group." I told Jody

and started walking toward them.

"Hi guys. Did you save us seats?" I brazenly asked.

At the table was Alex, Terry, Mathew and Mitchell.

Mitchell also worked the second shift with them. Alex

pulled out the chair next to him that was empty. There were

two empty chairs next to him and I knew that he had saved

them for us. "Thanks." I sat down and Jody sat next to me.

I looked around at the table they all had beer. "I'll be right back." I walked up to the bar and got me and Jody two

beers and walked back to the table.

"Are you old enough to have that?" Terry asked

"I have ID." Was my only answer.

He just laughed and nodded his head at us. Two

more beers later during dinner and we were deciding where

to go now. Terry and Alex speak in code and I never am

sure what they are talking about.

"Place down Franklin." Alex said.

"Yeah, that is rockin." Terry replied.

Everyone pushed back from the table and we all

walked out together.

"Why don't you ride with me. Franklin can be a rough area at night. I will bring you back to your car later." Alex said to me.

"And what are you driving this time?" I smiled at him when I said it.

He smiled and shook his head. "Come on." I started walking with him and then realized that Jody wasn't with me.

"Where's Jody?"

"She's with Mitchell."

How did he notice that when I hadn't seen her walk out with him? He doesn't miss anything. I sent her a text.

You with Mitchell? You're going down to the club

on Franklin?

Isa

Right behind you guys.

Jody

I felt better confirming her whereabouts. I was

really hoping that my ID got me into this place and not

arrested in front of Alex. I was getting more anxious by the

minute. I understood what Alex meant when we pulled into

the parking lot. There were homeless people hanging out in

the parking lot asking for money. It was scary down here. I

walked close to him and he put his hand on the small of my

back and led me toward the club entrance. We walked to

the front of the line and Alex took his hand off of my back

to shake hands with the doorman.

"Alejandro. How the hell are you? Haven't seen

you in a while."

Alejandro? Was he just calling him that or is that

his given name and Alex was just a nickname? I like

Alejandro. I wonder if he would let me call him that.

"Hey man, how's it going? I've got some people

with me tonight." He motioned back with his head.

He looked back at our group and undid the rope to

let us pass. Alex shook his hand and thanked him. I think

he slipped him money with that handshake but I wasn't

sure. That was it. No waiting in line, no ID check, nothing.

How did he do that? I didn't care. I just wanted to dance.

We made our way through the crowd to a booth in the

back. Why wasn't this spot taken? The place is packed? We

all filed in and Terry went to the bar. A few minutes later

the waitress came over with drinks. She brought beer for

everyone and shots of Petrone Tequila. I knew how to do

this after serving many shots of this at the bar. She set

down a cup of limes and a saltshaker. We each took one

and got ready. Alex and Terry didn't salt up their hands.

"Don't you want salt?" I asked him.

"No, straight up is good for me." He smiled down at me.

We all held up our shot glasses.

"Salud!" We all said in unison and drank down our shots. It burned all the way down but Alex and Terry didn't seem phased at all. I could see Alex watching me with a grin. I wanted to dance and was bouncing around in the seat to every song. I saw Alex grin up at Terry and then he took my hand. "Come on, let's dance." He pulled me out to the dance floor. Pitbull was playing and the floor was packed. He pulled my hips close and we started moving to the music. Suddenly Terry was behind me and he was up against me too moving in unison with us. I was sandwiched between them moving to the music. This was totally erotic

and oh was it fun. The song ended and Terry leaned over

and whispered into my ear. "For a white girl you sure can

move." I threw my head back and laughed. Alex grabbed

my waist and we kept dancing as Terry went back to the

table. I saw Jody and Mitchell dancing too. After a few

songs we sat down sweating and laughing. I have never

seen Alex so unreserved. Eventually other people from the

hospital made their way in. They had been waiting in line

like everyone else. We went and danced again. Terry

grabbed someone from work to dance with that I

recognized but I didn't really know her. Jody and Mitchell

were dirty dancing at this point and Mathew was with a

group from work. We danced and drank and had every

intention of staying until close. It was the most fun that I

have had in a long time, maybe ever. I excused myself and

went to the bathroom. When I came out of the stall Alex's

girlfriend was waiting for me at the sink. I just looked at

her and didn't say anything. What was she doing here? Did

she see me dancing with Alex and got mad?

"Hi, I am Susana."

"Isabella." I held out my hand and she just looked at

me.

"I just wanted to see what his new infatuation was."

She turned and walked away.

I stood there stunned. New infatuation? What was

she talking about? Were they not together anymore? When

I walked out of the bathroom Alex was standing at the

door. He grabbed my arm and pushed me to the corner.

"What did she say to you?" He asked with anger and

urgency.

"Nothing. She just introduced herself and said she

wanted to see what your new infatuation was. That's it,

then she left."

He looked me in the eyes for what felt like minutes.

"Are you sure? Is that all she said to you?"

"Yes Alex, I promise, that's all she said. What's wrong? What did you think would happen? Is she still your girlfriend?"

"No Isa, she isn't my girlfriend anymore. Are you sure you are okay?"

I put my hand on his cheek. "Alex, I am fine. Really. But are you okay? What happened? You two were together a long time."

"I am fine. Are you sure that is all that she said to you, because if she starts any shit with you I will…," he didn't finish his sentence. He just looked at me with those serious brown eyes and then took my hand to led me back to the table.

We closed the bar and all walked out together. I gave Jody a hug and told her that I would see her at work later, since it was Friday already. I wasn't sure if she was even going home, I had a feeling that her and Mitchell may hook up tonight. Good for her. She deserved a good man in her life. I got into Alex's truck and we left. He turned on the radio but we didn't go back to the restaurant. "Where are we going?" I asked with apprehension.

"I am driving you home. You have had too much to drink to drive."

"How do you know where I live?"

He didn't answer but took me right to mine and Tim's house. That's weird but obviously he isn't going to tell me how he knew I lived here now. "Thank you. I had fun."

"Me too."

I got out and walked up to the door. He backed out and left before I even got the door opened. I stumbled into bed clearly buzzed. Tim was asleep in bed.

Tim got up in the morning and was making an exorbitant amount of noise. I rolled over in bed and covered my head with the pillow. I tried to ignore him but I suddenly felt sick to my stomach. Oh man, I didn't think that I drank that much, but I definitely was going to vomit. I ran to the bathroom and threw up. I laid down on the cool floor. I feel awful. Worse than awful. I heard Tim leave the house. He didn't check on me, he didn't say a word, he just left for work. Great, now he is mad at me. That is just what I need. And how am I going to get my car before work? I crawled back to bed a couple of hours later with a soda in hand and fell asleep. At about three in the afternoon I got up and checked my phone. There was nothing. I sent a text to Tammy.

Can you take me to pick up my car?

Isa

Where is your car?

T

At Club 21 on Oracle.

Why is it there?

Went to a dinner, drank too much to drive it home.

Oh, Tim okay with that?

Why was she always worried about how Tim was
feeling about everything?

Don't know. He left this morning without saying a word to me.

I will be there in 30.

I got up and showered. I put on my Patty's t-shirt since I would drive into work right from the restaurant. When she got there I slid into the passenger seat. "Thanks for coming to get me."

"Sure. Must have been a good party."

I smiled thinking about the dancing that I did with Alex last night. I grinned sheepishly. "Yeah, it was fun." We arrived to where my car was parked. "Thanks again, I appreciate your help." Before I got out I asked, "What do you know about Brenda?"

"I don't know. What do you want to know?"

"I am not sure. Tim came home really late and trashed one night and the message on his phone in the morning was from her asking him if he got home okay. Isn't she married? What would she be doing out at three in the morning with Tim?"

"I don't know Isabella. She is separated from Martin though."

I just looked at her. "Really? Why?"

She shrugged her shoulders. "I don't know but I know they split. He went to Phoenix with the kids."

"He took the kids? Don't you think that is odd?"

"Why would it be odd?"

"Because the kids usually stay with the mom unless there is some kind of neglect or abuse."

"Really? How would you know this?"

"I have a lot of friends with divorced parents."

"I don't know what to say Isabella."

"You don't have to say anything. Thanks again." I slid out of the car and got into mine and went to work.

My shift went by and right on queue Alex and company came in. Alex didn't totally ignore me this time though. He walked up behind me and put his hand on the small of my back. I don't know why that sends a shiver up

my spine but it does. He got close to my ear and said,

"How are you feeling?"

I looked down and flushed. I turned my face toward

him and said in a low voice, "The morning wasn't pretty,

but I am on the mend."

"You're not in too much trouble I hope."

He was talking about Tim of course. "I am not sure

yet."

He frowned a little and nodded understanding my

lack of commitment to that answer. "You want to bring us a

round?"

"I will let Michelle know you are ready." He had turned and was walking away when I asked, " Petrone tonight?"

When I said that and stopped and walked back up to me. He put his lips near my ear and said, "I only do that with you."

My mouth dropped. I knew that wasn't true but I enjoyed the flirtation. He turned around and walked over to his group of friends. I went and let Michelle know they were ready for a round. As the night went on I watched Alex closer. He was very good at pool and rarely lost. He was always low key. Some of the other guys got loud and boisterous as the night went on but not him. He wasn't the same relaxed Alex that he was last night though. He was

watching and observing his surroundings tonight. Every

once in a while he would glance my way but I would

pretend that I didn't notice. I was going to miss seeing him

next week since it was Thanksgiving and I didn't have any

clinicals at the hospital. My mind drifted off to Tim and the

upcoming holiday. Tim and I couldn't seem to get along

about what to do for Thanksgiving. I want to go to my

mom's and he wants to go to Vegas to be with his family. I

told him he will never make it non-reving over the holiday

but he insists on trying. Whatever, I am not spending my

holiday in an airport. I wonder what Alex and Terry are

doing for Thanksgiving? I will have to remember to ask them when I have a chance.

The night finally came to a close and I noticed that they never made Alex and Terry leave when the bar locked the doors but their friends would go on without them. For some unknown reason they let them hang around while we all cleaned up and closed up. Alex and Terry shot pool and we were all doing our nightly chores. When we were finished I grabbed my purse and waited for Jody. We always walked out together. Alex and Terry walked out with us tonight. They made sure we got to our cars safely and then they retreated to theirs.

When I got home Tim wasn't there again. I know that he is mad but this is ridiculous. I was too tired to worry about it and went to bed. Maybe the holiday apart would be good for us.

Chapter 21

The next morning Tim was in bed sleeping. I didn't even here him come in last night. I got up and made some coffee. As I was sitting and enjoying the morning my phone buzzed. It was Jody.

Mitchell and I are going shooting with the guys. Do you want to come?

Jody

I didn't even know that Jody knew how to shoot or even liked it for that matter.

Shoot what?

Isa

Very funny. Guns of course. I guess they do this together a couple times a month.

Jody

Do you know how?

Isa

No, I just thought it would be fun.

Jody

Where at?

Isa

Jenson's at 10:00.

Jody

Okay, why not. See you there.

Isa

I got up and headed for the shower. I kind of just wanted to hang out with Alex. I could care less about shooting guns. How bad could it be? I jumped in the shower and started my routine. I started feeling queasy as I shaved my legs meticulously. All of the sudden I vomited. What was that all about? I cooled the shower down and let the water hit my face. I started to feel better already. It must be something I ate last night. I finished getting ready and left a note on the table for Tim.

I made my way for Jenson's and circled the parking lot until I saw a familiar vehicle. I saw Jody's so I parked near her and got out. I went inside feeling a little nervous. I have never been to a shooting range before. I spotted Alex before I saw Jody. He was firing off a round already right

next to Terry. Jody spotted me and waived me over.

Mitchell was teaching her how to hold the gun. I walked up

and observed. She aimed and fired. He gave her a .22

caliber semi automatic hand gun. She didn't do too bad for

her first round of shots. Then Mitchell took the gun and

reloaded for himself. Alex had spotted me and waved me

over.

"Ready to try a round?"

I nervously looked up at him. "Sure, I guess. I don't

know a thing about guns though."

Alex gave me all of the ins and outs of his .45 semi-

automatic pistol. When he was done instructing me he slid

a cartridge into the chamber. I aimed and fired multiple times. It didn't kick as much as I thought it would. I was a little wild on the target though. Alex took the gun and reloaded it for himself. He put five into the chest and five into the head of the paper dummy with precision. I was impressed. "Who taught you to shoot like that?"

"I practice a lot." Alex said with a sheepish grin.

We stayed for a couple of hours and then we all decided that lunch was in order. We went to Patty's of course since this had become our hang out. Alex led us to "his corner". We all ordered and Alex challenged us to some pool.

"No way, I have seen you play. You will take all of my money." I said to him laughing. The boys decided to play each other since there were four of them and none of the girls wanted to play. I watched Jody and Mitchell. They seemed so happy together. I think they have spent every minute together since the dinner. My phone buzzed and I looked down at it. It was from Tim and he was clearly angry.

DO YOU NOT UNDERSTAND WHAT CAN HAPPEN TO YOUNG GIRLS AT SHOOTING RANGES!!! WHAT ARE YOU THINKING!

That is obnoxious. What is going to happen to me? I am with my friends and four of them are men who are obviously experienced with guns. I replied.

Tim I understand your concern but really I am fine. The guys I work with are experienced marksmen. Don't worry. I will be home after lunch.
Isa

He went silent. The look on my face must have given me away and I didn't notice Alex watching me. He is always watching everything actually.

"What's going on Isa?" It was more of a statement then a question.

"Just talking to Tim."

"I could tell."

"How can you tell?" I challenged him.

"You get the same look on your face when you are talking to him."

 "What look?"

"Sadness."

I didn't expect that answer. Do I look sad when I talk to him? Maybe I should think about that. Maybe this was all a mistake. We do seem to fight a lot.

After lunch I headed back home as promised. Tim's car was gone when I got there. How mature to take off when you know that I am coming home, I thought to myself. I was tired and went to take a nap. I woke up an hour later and started my homework. There was still no sign of Tim. I thought about calling Tammy to see if she knew where he might hide but thought better of it. How would she know where to find him?

Later in the evening I heard Tim's car pull up. Finally, I thought to myself. Tim came in. "Hi there stranger. Where have you been hiding all day?" I said jokingly.

"What the hell is that supposed to mean? I am not hiding from you. You are the one out gallivanting around." He snapped at me.

"Whoa, down boy. I was joking Tim. What's wrong? Is this still about me coming in late from the Tech Dinner? Because you have barely spoken to me since then."

"It's about everything Isabella."

My heart started beating fast. He was going to ask me to leave. Why did this bother me? Wasn't I just considering this option anyway? "What do you mean everything?"

"You don't think. Can't you see that those men you work with just want to get into your pants?"

Oh no, not this conversation again. Why does he think this about every man that I am around? "Really Tim? Are we going to accuse all of my male friends of this?"

"You are stupid Isabella. I am a man, I know what they are capable of."

"Well I think you are wrong."

We went silent, clearly at an impasse. "Tim, do you want me to leave? Is this not working for you?"

"I think it's not working for you. I will need some time to think about this over Thanksgiving."

I nodded in agreement. "Okay, we will talk about this again after you have time to think." Tim walked out of the room and went to take a shower. I stayed at the table thinking about my options and what would really make me happy.

Chapter 22

The week dragged on. It was torture being in a house with someone who wouldn't talk to you. I told Jody about the conversation and she thought it was weird and unhealthy. I was starting to think she was right. She thinks that I should dump Tim and go for Alex. She thinks he wants me. I informed her that Alex thinks of me as a little sister or something but nothing more. I am not glamorous enough for him.

Thanksgiving day was here and I was happy to be going to my mom's. She was disappointed that Tim wouldn't be joining us but understood why it is important to him to go home for the holidays. It was nice to be at the table again with mom and dad. It was the most relaxed that I had been in weeks. All of my friends had places to go so I had no strays to bring home for turkey this year. After dinner I went to my old room for a nap. I must have slept for two hours before I rejoined my family in the living room. I sat watching TV with them and then sent a mass text out to Alex, Terry, Mathew, Jody and Mitchell.

Anyone want to come over for a movie? I'm in the

mood for Pulp Fiction.

Isa

I was shocked when everyone said they were in. I kissed

my parents good night and thanked them for a fabulous

dinner and headed home. I was unloading my left overs that

mom packed when Jody and Mitchell pulled up. We went

in and popped popcorn and pulled the movie up on Netflix.

It wasn't long before Alex, Mathew and Terry arrived. I

offered drinks to everyone. Tim always has beer in the

refrigerator thankfully and a bottle of Jagermeister. We all

had a beer and a shot and then sat down to watch the

movie. Mathew kept pouring shots periodically during the movie. I didn't realize that I was drunk until it was too late. The movie ended and Jody and Mitchell left with Mathew right behind them. That left me, Alex and Terry. We started watching a stand up comedian on TV. I excused myself and went to the bathroom. I came out and Alex was standing there. "Are you alright?" Why was I always the one who was tipsy or drunk and he was always alright?

I giggled and said, "Yeah, I am fine." I took a step closer to him while looking him in the eye. "Why don't you stay?" I couldn't believe that just came out of my mouth. The liquor had taken over and I was no longer in control of my senses. I put arms around his neck. He picked me up around the waist and carried me into the bedroom

and laid me down. He leaned down next to my ear and said,

"Not like this Isa." He turned and walked out quietly

closing the door behind him. I must have passed out after

that.

When I woke up in the morning it was to throw up.

I barely made it to the bathroom. I threw up two more times

before I attempted to go to the kitchen for a soda. While I

was there my cell phone rang. "Hello?"

"I just wanted to make sure that you were okay."

Alex softly said.

"Can you hang on a minute?" I ran to the bathroom

and vomited yet again. I am sure that Alex could hear. How

nice, I thought, just what he wants to hear. I got back on the phone. "Sorry. I am doing okay."

"I'll be there in a few minutes," was all he said and then he hung up.

I stayed in the bathroom knowing what was coming. The doorbell rang about twenty minutes later. I was able to make my way to the door in order to let Alex in. He walked in carrying Menudo, 7-up, Bitters and Tabasco. I just looked at him as he put the Menudo on the stove and grabbed a glass to mix his secret concoction of 7-Up, Bitters and Tabasco. "Sit." He told me. I did what I was ordered to do. He set the glass in front of me. "One sip every ten minutes." I took my first sip. It wasn't great but wasn't bad either. He prepared the Menudo in two bowls and placed bread in the center of the table. "Eat."

"I can't eat Menudo feeling like this."

"Non-sense, this is the best cure for a hangover. I am Latin, I know."

I laughed and slowly began sipping the broth and eating the bread. I took my sips of hang over concoction as directed and before long I was at least feeling human. "Alex, thank you."

"You're welcome. Come on let's find a movie to watch."

We curled up together on the couch and found a Netflix movie on demand to watch. I fell asleep but he sat with me anyway and watched the movie. I woke up a couple of

hours later and he was still there with me on the couch. I

smiled up at him. "You're still here."

"Yes I am. When is Tim coming back from Vegas?"

"Sunday night."

He looked at me saying nothing and I wondered

what he was thinking about. "I better go. Are you okay to

be alone?"

"If I say no will you stay?'

He smiled at me and kissed my forehead. "No, I

will call Jody to come stay with you."

"Don't do that. She will bring Mitchell and I will never get any rest." We both laughed knowing what I was implying. I walked Alex to the door and he left.

Chapter 23

I didn't get out of bed much over the next two days. I was just not recovering as well as I usually do. Maybe I have the flu. I didn't even hear Tim come home Sunday night. That wasn't very nice of me to not wait up for him but I just couldn't stay awake. I had school the next morning and left him another note on the table. "Welcome home. I hope your holiday was good. Miss you, Isabella."

I got to class and sat down. I looked as green as I felt. Jody looked at me and said, "You don't look so good. Are you okay?"

I nodded no and then left to go throw up. I did this two more times during the day. Finally Jody said to me, "Don't get mad at me for asking this, because I hate this analogy, but are you pregnant?"

I smiled and said, "Of course not. I am on the pill, and besides you need to have sex to get pregnant and Tim hasn't gotten near me in a month."

"Are you sure? You didn't miss any pills?"

I stared at her not answering.

"You need to pee on a stick girlfriend. We are going to the store after class."

"I can't do it at my house." Was all I could get out.

"Then we will go to mine, but you need to know for sure."

The next class took forever and I couldn't focus on any of it. We made our way out to our cars and I followed Jody to the nearest drug store. We went in and picked out two different pregnancy tests. I paid and then we made our way to her house. I was nervous. I sat in her kitchen drinking water insisting that I didn't need to go just yet. Jody sat with me. Thank goodness her dad wasn't home.

"Just do it and get it over with."

I sighed and grabbed the bag and went to the bathroom. A few minutes later I heard a knock on the bathroom door.

"Isabella? Are you okay in there?"

I didn't answer because I was trying to sob quietly.

"Can I open the door?"

I opened it for her and handed her the two sticks. One had a plus mark and the other had a blue line. I was definitely pregnant. She looked at them and then at me. "I take it this isn't good news."

I started crying again and she hugged me.

"Jody, I am not even sure if I like him let alone raise a child with him. What are my parents going to say? They will want me to marry him and I don't want to marry him!"

She rubbed my back and said, "Then don't marry him. You don't have to. You don't have to make any decisions right now."

"Please don't tell anyone. I need to think this through. I don't want everyone to know. Please?"

"Of course not. It isn't my news to tell. I am here for you, okay?"

I nodded knowing that she would be here for me no matter what.

"I should probably get going. Thank you Jody."

She hugged me again and I left. I tried to not cry on the way home so Tim wouldn't be suspicious. I didn't want to tell him just yet. I want time to think first.

When I got home I muttered a hello and went to the bedroom to lie down. I was so tired and just needed to rest. Tim didn't seem to care and sat in front of the television until he went to bed later.

The next few weeks were more of the same. We didn't talk much and he was either in front of the television or out late. I secretly bought some vitamins to take care of my baby and wondered if my previous drinking escapades had hurt my little one. I was torn about what to do. I couldn't do adoption because I knew that as soon as I had my baby I would want it. I didn't want to get an abortion because it isn't my baby's fault that I wasn't responsible or prepared for this. I could choose to not tell Tim and go have my baby on my own, but would it be fair for my baby to not know its father? I could stay with Tim and raise the baby. Give it a family that celebrates holidays and birthdays together and gathers around the dinner table at night. That sounds great but Tim and I hardly talk now, can you imagine what a baby will do to the relationship? I decided for now to make a doctor's appointment. I need to take care of this little life growing inside of me.

Chapter 24

The Christmas party for Radiology was this

Saturday. I reminded Tim earlier in the week, and I was

shocked that he agreed to go. I felt fat already and stood

there staring sideways into the bathroom mirror. I have no

idea what I am going to wear to it. Something black. Black

is slimming. I started combing through my closet and

picked out a loose fitting, long black dress. That should do.

I still don't know what I am going to do about the baby. I

think about it all of the time, well at least when I'm not

sleeping.

We drove to the party in relative silence. When we

walked into the ballroom we both smiled and put on a show

of being a happy couple. Why am I going through all of

this work? It really shouldn't be this hard to be with

someone. I scanned the room and found Jody and Mitchell.

She had saved us seats. We sat and Jody and I started

chatting. Tim looked around seeming very restless.

Eventually Alex, Terry and his date, and Mathew and his

date all showed up and sat at our table. We were all talking

and laughing when I noticed that Tim had gotten up from

the table and gone somewhere. I wonder where he is?

Mitchell came back with drinks and I nursed my water. I

saw Alex eyeing me like usual. I wonder why he didn't

bring a date? I knew better then to engage in much

conversation because Tim would accuse them of 'wanting

to get into my pants' and I just don't have the energy for

that fight tonight. We all went and got food at the buffet

and still no Tim. The music started shortly after that and

everyone went to dance. Jody and Mitchell were so in love.

You could just tell with the way they looked at each other

and how gentle he was with her. I sighed wishing that were

me. My decision wouldn't be so hard if I had a relationship

like that. I sat staring at everyone and felt someone sit

down next to me. It was Alex.

"Where did Tim run off to?"

"That is a good question." I said feeling a little annoyed.

He didn't say anything else. He just sat with me people watching. That's what I love about Alex, we can just be together and it's comfortable.

"Are you the designated driver tonight?"

"What? Why?"

"You are nursing that water like it might run out."

My face felt hot. Only Alex would notice that I was drinking water tonight. Of course lately he has seen me throw back some serious booze and it probably did seem odd that I was now nursing a water.

"Yeah, it's my turn."

Terry came up and whispered something in Alex's ear. He was holding onto his date's hand as he talked to Alex.

"Where's Mathew?"

"He went upstairs to his room with his date. Apparently they have a room here for the night." Terry replied so we could all hear.

"And where's Tim?"

"Outside."

I looked between them frowning. "What happened? What does Tim have to do with Mathew going to his room with his girlfriend?"

Alex said, "Come with me," and he took my hand and led me out to the lobby of the hotel. "Isa, Tim hit on Mathew's girlfriend. Terry says that they had words about it. Tim stormed out and Mathew went up to his room out of respect to you. He didn't want to embarrass you with this."

"Hit on her how?"

"I don't know, I just know what Terry just told me."

"I don't believe it. Why would he do that here where he knows these are my friends?"

"I don't know Isa. I am sorry."

"You said that he was outside?"

"Yes."

"I guess I should go look for him. He is my ride home."

"I thought you were driving."

"Yeah but he has the keys." I went back to the table and got my purse. I said good night to everyone and headed outside. Alex did not follow me out, he stayed at the table with everyone. I made my way out the lobby doors and Tim was pacing on the sidewalk.

"Why don't you ever answer your God damn phone Isabella! I have been calling you so that we could leave."

"Why do you want to leave?"

"Because this party is lame, that's why."

"Did you hit on Mathew's girlfriend?"

"Is that what they told you? What bullshit Isabella. Why can't you see that?"

"If it's not true then tell me what happened? Tell me why my friends felt like they had to leave the party?"

He started walking toward the car. "I don't have to explain anything, you got that?"

I followed since I needed the ride home and didn't want anyone to come out and see us fighting. We got in the car and I started crying. This made him even angrier.

"Stop crying. You have nothing to cry about."

I have nothing to cry about? I have plenty to cry about. I decided to just let it out, let him know the reason I feel so sad right now. "I'm pregnant. I am pregnant and you

are unbearable to be around. Is that a good enough reason
for me to cry?" There, I said it.

He went perfectly still and stared straight ahead.
After several seconds he said, "What did you just say to
me?"

"I'm pregnant."

"Who's is it?"

"What? What the hell is that supposed to mean? It's
yours. Who else?"

He started the car and started backing out. "Oh I
don't know, one of the guys you work with maybe. You
may not even know which one at this point."

"You fucking asshole, how dare you talk to me like that! I have never cheated on you. I am not the one going around hitting on other people's girlfriends. I am not the one getting text messages from married women asking me if I got home okay. Who's doing the cheating around here?"

"What are you accusing me of Isabella?" He was driving now and much too fast.

"I am accusing you of fucking Brenda, that's what! Are you the reason she's separated? Did you break up that family?"

"Who told you that?'

"None of your damn business."

"Like hell, I want to know who is talking about me!"

"Take a look around you Tim. People can see what's going on." I am just talking now, trying to draw the truth out of him. What people have seen him? Nobody as far as I know.

He hit the steering wheel and didn't answer. I guess I figured out who he's been having sex with all of these weeks. Tears were still streaming down my face.

"Why did you lie to me about being on birth control? We haven't even had sex since like October. This is not my kid."

"I didn't lie to you. When you got mad at me for having dinner with Tony and broke up with me I stopped taking my pills. I wasn't expecting a reunion with you, and then we had sex remember? I started my pills again the next day but it was too late. I thought it would all be fine but I was wrong."

"I don't want a kid."

Wow, I didn't expect that cruel of a let down, but there it was. At least I have something to work with now. It's either on my own or not at all. I stopped talking and looked out the window. We said nothing else. When we got home I went into the bathroom and got ready for bed. I grabbed a pillow and a blanket and went out to the couch. I text Tammy even though it was late. I wanted to know if

she knew about this affair that he was having.

I know that Tim is having an affair with Brenda.

Isa

He told you?

T

Did you know?

Isa

Yes.

T

Why didn't you tell me?

Isa

I couldn't. Mike wouldn't let me. They are friends.

T

And I thought we were friends

Isa.

We are.

T

Not any more.

Isa

I snapped my phone shut and started crying again. She knew and didn't tell me. Now I am pregnant with his child and I hate him. I couldn't sleep and I turned on the television. I sat up all night staring at meaningless programs, trying to figure out where I was going to go. Where was I going to live? Do I keep this baby or not? Morning came and I heard Tim get up. I pretended to be asleep when he came out. He left the house and I got up and started packing. I pulled out my suitcases and started putting my clothes in. I found some boxes in the garage and brought them in. I didn't have a lot but I didn't want to have to come back for anything either. I started packing my

camera, computer, and school things into one of the boxes.

I went into the closet and pulled out my shoes and shoved

them in boxes. I accidently knocked a pair of Tim's dress

shoes onto the floor. I picked them up to put them back on

the rack and a baggy fell out onto the floor. I froze and just

stared down at it. It was full of white powder. I slowly bent

over and picked it up. I started thinking about his erratic

behavior and refusing to go in for his drug test. Is this

cocaine? How could I tell? I wasn't much of a drug user in

high school and had never done cocaine. I started thinking

about movies that had drug use. How do they know the

powder is really cocaine? I opened the baggy and put my

finger in it. I put my finger on my tongue. Holy shit, my

tongue just went numb. I got scared. I don't want to know

about this or have anything to do with this. Oh my God I

could be accused of being an accessory to drug use or

distribution. Who knows what he is in to. My heart was

beating so hard I could hear it in my ears. I just wanted to

get out of hear. I no longer cared if I had everything.

Suddenly I heard Tim's voice behind me.

        "What are you doing with that?" His voice was low

and angry.

        I spun around. My heart was beating so hard I could

hardly hear anything else.   I was clutching the baggie.

What am I going to do? Give it to him? Will he let me just leave if I do?

"Give it to me." He said slowly.

I continued to stare at him. I was trapped in the closet. I could hardly breath, my chest was heaving. I didn't want anything to do with this I just wanted to run. I was still clutching the baggie. It was still open from when I put my finger in it. I continued to stare at him almost hyperventilating by now. "What are you into Tim? Why do you have this?"

"GIVE IT TO ME!" He shouted coming close to my face. I was scared. What am I going to do? I don't know what to do.

I then threw the bag at him and the powder flew

everywhere. I didn't even know what hit me it all happened

so fast. I was up against the wall and my feet were

dangling. I couldn't breath. Tim had grabbed me by the

neck and was holding me up against the wall. I struggled,

kicking and pushing but I couldn't get him to budge.

"I will kill you for this you fucking bitch! I will kill

you!"

For the first time in my life I thought that I really

would die. Now my struggling was to get his hands off of

my neck. I needed a breath. Oh God, I can't breath. I

wiggled and kicked but I couldn't make him budge. I had

no idea he was this strong. The room started to go black

and I felt a punch to the side of my jaw and he dropped me.

I lay on the floor gasping for air. I couldn't take any in. My

throat felt closed, and then the kick to my belly came, and

another and another. I screamed out in pain and tried to

block him but he just kept kicking. I was screaming.

Screaming for him to stop as loud as I could and then it all

went silent.

Beep, beep, beep....

What is that noise? I hear voices, who is it? Oh

God, wonder if it is Tim? I have to escape, I have to get out

of here! I am struggling to move but I can't. He will kill

me, I have to get out of here.

"Nurse, nurse!" I hear a voice shout. Nurse? What nurse? Why can't I open my eyes?

Beep, beep, beep....

I hear that sound again. There are voices around me.

"I will kill him myself. What kind of man would do this to her?"

"Calm down Alex. This is how these guys are. You know that. Don't let your feelings for her cloud your judgment."

His feelings for her? Alex has feelings for who? Oh no, it's going black again.

Beep, beep, beep…

"I will sit with her, go, get something to eat at least Alex. Go."

Was that Jody? I need to tell her what I found, what happened. I can't speak. Why can't I speak? I feel her hand holding mine and I drift back off.

Beep, beep, beep….

Someone is crying. Who's crying? I can't see.

Beep, beep, beep…

I am sick of hearing the beeping. Why doesn't it stop?

"Isa? Isa, it's Alex. Try to wake up Isa. You are safe now. Open your eyes, please."

I am safe? Where am I? Why can't I open my eyes?

Beep, beep, beep…

There is more crying.

"Mrs. Weston I will sit with her. Go home and get some sleep. I will call you if there is change in her condition. I promise."

How does Alex know my mom? My mom, oh no, my mom knows what happened. She is the one that I hear crying.

Beep, beep, beep...

I open my eyes and look around. Where am I?

"Hello young lady."

It is Alex. Why is he here? I see him push the call light.

"Isa? Can you talk to me?" Alex asks softly as he touches my hand.

I smile a little at him but I still say nothing. I am stiff and in pain. My neck and throat are throbbing.

"It is good to see your beautiful green eyes again." He said with a grin. He is sitting at my side holding my hand.

I try to look around to see where I am. I am stiff and can hardly move. I bring my hand up to my belly. Alex looks down at me and his eyes are sad, so sad. I must be in worse condition then I think. I try to talk. My mouth is so dry and my throat is sore, so sore. I start to remember now. Tim was choking me. No wonder I am sore. I touch my throat. "Alex?"

"Shush, just rest for now. I will explain it all to you soon. You just need to get well right now."

The nurse walked in. "Well, look who is awake. My name is Tara and I will be your nurse for today. The doctor will be here soon to examine you. Are you having pain?

I shook my head yes.

"Can you rate your pain on a scale of one to ten with ten being the worst pain of your life?"

"About a five." I whispered. "I am just sore all over, mostly my head. What happened to me?"

"We'll let the doctor explain all of that to you."

Alex stood hovering over me. He had made a phone call when I was talking to the nurse. The nurse left the room after writing down some information from the

monitors.

"I called your mom to let her know that you were

awake. Your mom and dad will be here shortly."

"I don't want them to see me here." I was louder

now, almost frantic.

"Isa, they saw you the night you came in and every

day since. They know what happened. Your mom has been

crying at your bedside everyday."

"What exactly did happen? How many days have

gone by?"

Just then the doctor walked in. "Hello Isabella. I am

Dr. Young. I am the internist that is caring for you." He

shined a light in each eye as he spoke to me. "Do you remember what happened to you?"

I thought for a minute. I didn't want to talk about what I remembered. "Not exactly."

The doctor looked at me for a long moment. "Let me tell you what I know about you at this point. You came in as a trauma patient four days ago. When you arrived you had facial and neck bruising, a facial laceration and profuse pelvic bleeding."

Tears started running down my face. My baby was gone, he killed my baby. I stayed silent.

"You were not able to answer questions coherently but you were still conscious. You were put on oxygen and you were given blood due to a falling blood pressure and

inability to control the bleeding. One of the x-ray techs in

the trauma room recognized you and we were able to call

your parents to tell them what happened. Your friend Jody

arrived as well after your mom called her. She informed us

that you were pregnant. You were taken to the operating

room for a D & E. You have been heavily sedated for the

past several days to keep you comfortable and still while

we ascertained the possible injuries to you neck. I am

happy to report that your c-spine has been cleared, you

haven't needed any more blood and there are no other

internal injuries."

Tears were still rolling down my face. I said nothing.

"The police want to get a statement from you. Are you feeling up to that?'

"Not really. Does it have to be today?'

The doctor looked at Alex. Why did he look at Alex for the answer?

"The sooner the better Isa." Alex answered for him.

I could barely see him through the tears in my eyes. "I'm afraid."

"I know but the police need to know what happened in that house."

"Do I need a lawyer?" My voice broke as I asked the question.

"That is your prerogative of course, but you are not under arrest this is just a statement."

"How do you know that?"

"Know what?"

"That I am not under arrest?"

Alex said nothing. He stood there quietly.

"I want to talk to my mom first."

"Okay."

My mom and dad arrive about a half an hour later. I had fallen asleep again but awoke when my mom touched my hand. I started crying as soon as I saw my mom. "Mom, I am so sorry. I am sorry that I disappointed you. I am sorry." I sobbed. I could hardly talk.

"Shhh, calm down Isabella. We are just happy that you are okay."

"The police want to talk to me mom. I am scared. Should I get a lawyer first? What do I do mom?"

"Did you do anything wrong?"

"No, but wonder if they don't believe me. Wonder if they believe Tim?"

"They are looking for Tim, Isabella. They haven't found him yet."

"How did they find me then?"

"The neighbors called the police when they heard you screaming." My mom explained. "Do you still want a lawyer Isabella?"

"I didn't do anything wrong. I was packing my things to leave and I accidently found the drugs. He walked up behind me and scared me. I threw it at him and the cocaine went everywhere. That's when he started choking me." I was crying with deep sobs. I could hardly catch my breath in between words.

"Then that's what the police need to know." My mom stated calmly.

I shook my head in agreement.

My mom looked at Alex and he nodded. My parents left the room and an officer came in. "My name is officer Green. I need to get a statement from you and ask you some questions."

I nodded in agreement.

He then looked up at Alex. "Could you step outside while we talk?"

"I'd rather stay." Alex then flashed a badge at the officer.

"What's your name and department officer?"

"Alejandro Ortiz, DEA."

"Badge number?"

"1313"

"Can I have a look at that?" The officer confirmed Alex's badge and identification.

My head was spinning. Alex is DEA? I thought he was a fellow x-ray student who just graduated? Was he investigating Tim and me? Did he know that Tim was in possession of drugs? My heart was beating hard. I participated in underage drinking in front of him. Will he arrest me for it?

The officer turned back to me and set up a recorder. "Can you state your name?"

"Isabella Weston."

"How old are you?"

"19"

"Where do you live?"

"Up until four days ago I lived at 1425 Camino de Oeste."

"Do you live alone?"

"No, I was living with my boyfriend, Tim Tovar."

"Tell me what happened the morning of Sunday, December 12th."

I took a deep breath before I started. I made no eye contact with Alex. I focused on officer Green. "We had attended a Christmas party the night before. We had gotten into a fight because he had reportedly hit on one of my coworkers girl friends at the party. We left early as a result and started fighting in the car. I started crying and he got angrier. He said to stop crying, that I didn't have anything

to cry about." I took another deep breath and then

continued. "I told him that I was pregnant." I briefly

glanced at Alex and quickly looked away embarrassed that

he was hearing all of this.

"Then what?"

Tears started rolling down my face. "He wanted to

know whose baby it was? I was angry and asked him who

else's baby would it be? He said he thought that I was

messing around with men that I work with. I told him that

wasn't true and that the baby was his. He said how since

we hadn't had sex in weeks. I told him that I had gone off

of birth control when he had broken up with me in October.

When we reunited I started my pills again but it was already too late. He then told me that he didn't want a baby."

"He stated that he didn't want a baby?"

"Yes."

"Go on."

"When we got home I slept on the couch and he slept in the bedroom. He left early the next morning and I got up and started packing my things. I just wanted to leave and never come back."

"Where were you going to go?"

"I was going to go home and explain this mess to my parents."

"Did they know that you were coming?"

"No."

"Go on."

"I packed my clothes in my suit cases and found some boxes in the garage for the rest of my things. I went into the closet to pack my shoes. I accidently knocked over Tim's dress shoes. I picked them up and when I did a baggie fell out onto the floor. I picked it up and saw that it had white powder in it."

"How much?"

"I don't know. Maybe a quarter of the bag was full?"

"Then what happened? I put my finger in the powder and touched my tongue with it to see if it was cocaine."

"Why did you think that would tell you if it was cocaine?"

"I don't know. I never did drugs and all I know is what I have seen on TV."

He continued to stare at me so I kept talking. "My tongue went numb when I touched my finger to my tongue." He still said nothing. "Then I heard Tim's voice behind me. He asked me what I was doing with the bag? I didn't even hear him come in let alone walk in behind me. I turned and looked at him. I was scared. I was scared of him, I was scared of the drugs, and I panicked. He said to

give him the bag. I threw it at him and the cocaine flew

everywhere." I was crying again. "The next thing I

remember I was dangling up against the wall." I sobbed

and struggled to catch my breath. "He had me by the neck.

I could not get away. I pushed and wiggled and kicked but I

couldn't break free. I couldn't breath. He said that he would

kill me and I really thought at that moment he would. Then

he hit me in the face with his free hand and dropped me on

the floor. I still couldn't get any air in me. I was gasping so

hard but I couldn't get any air and then, and then, he kicked

me. I screamed and then it all went black. I don't remember

anything else."

"Do you know where Tim may have gotten the drugs?"

"No, I didn't even know that he did drugs. I was suspicious a few weeks ago though when his work called to tell him to come in for a random drug test and he refused to go. He said that everyone could miss one. I don't know if he ever did get tested."

"Where does Tim work?"

"Union Air."

"I want you to make list of friends, relatives, enemies anyone that may know where he is."

"Okay." I glanced over at Alex. His fists were clenched tight and his face looked angry. Was he mad at me? At my stupidity?

Officer Green turned off the recorder. "Tim is currently wanted for assault and battery. I am sure there will be further charges after the DA reviews your statement and other interviews are conducted. If he contacts you try to listen for noises in the background for a possible location and see if he will give you his location. Here is my card if you think of anything else that I should know."

"There is something else that I forgot."

Officer Green turned the recorder on. I found out that he was having an affair with a girl he works with. Her husband is a cop and I am told that they just separated and he moved to Phoenix. Her name is Brenda and her husbands name is Martin. I don't know her last name but she works for Union Air as well."

"We'll check it out and see if she knows his whereabouts." He clicked the recorder off again and this time looked over at Alex. He stood up and thanked me for my statement and left with Alex right behind him. My parents returned to the room.

"Mom, can you call Patty's and tell them I can't work this Saturday?"

"Jody already took care of that honey."

"Where are my things?"

"Alex collected your suitcases and the boxes that you did have packed. They were searched before he was able to remove them from the house, and then he brought them to the house for us. I don't know if you have anything else over there."

"I am not sure either. I am sure that whatever got left behind can be replaced some other time."

My dad hadn't said a word since he arrived with mom. He looked distraught and I felt guilty. My parents didn't deserve this.

"Mom, have they said when I can go home?"

"I don't know honey. They haven't said."

I felt wiped out already and I had only been awake for a little over an hour. I closed my eyes and drifted off to sleep again.

I open my eyes and I can't breath. His hand is squeezing my throat closed. I pull and scratch at him. I am dying, he will never let go. I kick at him. I have to save my baby. I have to get to my baby.

"Isabella! Wake up, wake up, it's okay." Alex has me by the shoulders trying to get me to hear him. I open my eyes and stare at him. Trying to comprehend who I am looking at. I am scared and my breathing is heavy. My forehead is dripping with sweat. "It's okay, I am right here."

I look around. It is nighttime. "Where are my

parents?"

"They went home for the night. I told them I would

be here with you." Alex sat down on the side of the bed. He

smoothed my hair back from my face. I closed my eyes

when he touched my face.

"Alex, who are you?"

He looked puzzled at me. "What do you mean?"

"Who are you?" I said louder almost frantic. "I

thought you were an x-ray tech, but you are a DEA agent

named Alejandro Ortiz?"

He shook his head in agreement and sighed. "Yes, I

am a DEA agent and yes, I am a x-ray tech. My full name

is Alejandro Xavier Ortiz. I am from Douglas, AZ. My mother was born and raised in Douglas and my dad is from Agua Prieta, Mexico. He is a legal alien here in the United States. Nobody but you and Terry know that I am an agent. I took this assignment because my schooling would be paid and I would have another career to fall back on when I am through with DEA."

"I don't understand. Why would your schooling be paid for? What assignment?"

"Isabella, I can't tell you everything. I have already told you too much and I need to know that our conversation won't leave this room."

I shook my head. "I won't tell anybody."

"The DEA frequently puts agents within hospitals and airports because that is where drug diversion is easiest and accessible. In order to be within the hospital you need to have a skill or license to support a role here. I chose x-ray and the department supported it."

"Why would you think that you would not stay DEA for the rest of your career?"

Alex put his face in his hands and then pulled his hands down and looked at me. "Isabella, this job can be very dangerous." He stopped. "I thought that I would have a family someday and I don't want them in any danger or worrying about whether I am coming home after an assignment."

"I understand." I looked down at my hands and then I smiled slightly. "I guess that explains your marksmanship."

He laughed with me.

"I have to do regular target practice. It's part of the job."

"Terry was pretty good too." I looked at him questioning.

"Yes he is and there is a reason for that."

"Your partner?"

"Yes."

I thought quietly for a while. "Are you working my case?"

"Not officially. I am too close to you to do that objectively, but I am aloud to hear the progress of the case."

"Isabella, I have to ask you something."

I looked up at him and felt anxiety at what he needed to know.

"Did Tim ever bring home any suitcases from the airport?"

"Not that I know of. Why?"

"They found a suitcase full of marijuana in the house. It is an unmarked suitcase with tags on it to be delivered to Tucson on Union Air. It is thought that it was sent with the intent for him to pick it up or that someone missed a drop and he took it for himself."

I was teary again. "Alex, please believe me when I tell you that I have no idea."

He nodded and stared at me.

"Alex?"

He kept looking at me.

"Will he come after me?"

"I don't know. When you are released I am going to take you downtown to get a restraining order."

"Okay."

We sat quietly for a few minutes and then he took my hand and kissed it. "I am so glad that you are okay. I was so afraid that you were not going to make it there for a little while."

I felt choked up again and continued to look at him with moist eyes. I didn't know what to say.

"I feel empty Alex. I feel sad and empty like I am never going to be able to stop crying."

"I understand."

I looked away. He couldn't understand. How could any man understand what it is like to lose a baby?

"Isabella." I turned my face toward him again. "I really do understand." I stared at him and nodded my head. "Listen to me, I understand." He stood up and walked to the window. I looked at him confused. Why is he frustrated? "Do you remember when I came back from Cancun?" He said with his back still toward me.

"Yes."

"You asked me if I was okay. Do you remember that?"

"Yes."

"Why did you ask me that?"

"I don't know. I could just feel it when I was near you. I could feel that you were angry or sad."

"And I can feel your sadness right now." He turned and looked at me. His face pained, almost distraught. "I went to Cancun with Susana." He paused. "I took her there to propose to her."

My eyes were huge. He proposed to her? My heart sank. I don't know why but it hurt even worse.

"I proposed because she was pregnant and I wanted us to be a family."

Now I really felt ill. They are going to have a baby? I can't do this. Not when I just lost mine. I wanted to tell him to stop but he looked so desperate. I let him keep talking.

"I rented a boat and we were cruising the coastline at sunset. I popped the question and gave her the ring. She took it and put it on, and then she said to me, 'I don't know if you will still want to marry me now.' I asked her what she meant and she said, 'I got rid of the baby.' Just like that

Isabella. She aborted my baby without asking me, without telling me, without giving me a choice. I would have raised that child on my own if she didn't want it. I would have paid for everything but I didn't get the chance. I took the ring and threw it into the ocean. I flew back that night and left her there."

I was crying again. All I have done since I woke up was cry. I was sobbing. Sobbing for me, sobbing for Alex, sobbing for our dead babies. I held my hand out to him and he walked back over to the bed and took it. I pulled him to me and hugged him. "I am sorry Alex. I am so sorry." I said in between crying and breathing. He held me for what felt like forever. He lay down on his side and cradled my head to his chest.

"I am too." He said and rubbed my hair back from my face.

When I finally stopped crying I looked up at him. His big brown eyes looked back at me. It was the most comfort I had felt in a long time. Just as I was drinking him in the door opened and Alex jumped up. It was Jody, Mitchell and Terry.

Jody paused at the door. "Am I interrupting?"

"No, come on in." Alex said looking uncomfortable at being caught embracing me on the bed.

They all came in and kissed and hugged me. Jody brought a big bouquet of flowers, which really did cheer me up.

Terry looked sheepishly between Alex and me. He's as intuitive as Alex I swear. We all sat and talked and laughed a little too. It was nice to be with everyone again even if it was in a hospital room. Mitchell was excited about his upcoming bike race. It goes from Bisbee to Douglas and back again. He went into great detail about his training and his new bike. Jody has been doing some riding with him but complained that she just can't keep up with him. Everyone left about nine, everyone except for Alex. Terry offered to stay with me but Alex refused and said that he wasn't going to leave whether he stayed or not. Terry

gave me a kiss on the cheek and whispered in my ear, "He

is crazy about you." I blushed not expecting that secret to

be spilled by his friend. I smiled and he winked at me. Jody

and Mitchell followed and said that they would see me

tomorrow.

Chapter 25

After everyone left Alex and I sat quietly. "Have
you stayed with me every night since I have been here?"

"Yes."

"Where do you sleep?"

"In the chair. It reclines."

I frowned and then held my hand out to him again.
He walked over looking confused as to what I wanted. I
slid over and patted the bed. "Lay down with me." He
looked hesitant at me. "I won't violate you, I promise." I
laughed and he rolled his eyes. He sat down on the side of

the bed and looked at me for a few moments. I pulled on

his hand. "Come on I am tired." He lay down next to me

and I turned on my side. He put his arm over me and I

snuggled up against him. Having him that close to me,

feeling him behind me made me excited. I always feel that

way when I am close to Alex though. I closed my eyes and

fell into a restful sleep. I felt happy for the first time in a

long time.

We didn't move all night and the nurse cleared her

throat loudly at the bedside at seven in the morning. She

was not happy to see Alex in the bed with me. It was

borderline even letting him stay let alone sleep with me. I

looked at her and smiled. "I asked him to lay with me so I could sleep. It's not his fault."

She didn't say anything, just waited for him to move. He got up and stretched. He looked so good. I could wake up to that everyday for sure, I thought to myself. I almost felt guilty thinking about Alex like that after just getting out of an abusive relationship. I don't want Alex to think he is my rebound man. I looked back at the nurse. "Can I go home today?"

"We will see what the doctor says when he comes to see you this morning." She took my vital signs and excused Alex to check my pad to assess if the bleeding had slowed down. He returned after she left. "Are you hungry? Do you want a coffee or anything?"

"Coffee is good."

"I will run to Starbucks and then I will be right back. Do not leave this room, got it?"

"Got it." I said and saluted.

He was only gone a few minutes and the door opened again. I started to say that was fast but stopped when I saw who it was. Tammy walked in and looked at me timidly.

"How are you doing?" She asked me.

My heart was racing. Did Tim know she was here? Would she tell him?

"Fine. I am fine." I tried to sound confident and strong.

She stood a safe distance from the bed. "Good, I am glad. I am sorry about what happened."

"What exactly happened Tammy? Who told you what happened?"

She looked stunned. Not expecting me to lash out at her. "Mike told me. Tim didn't show up to work and then Greg told him that the police had come by and asked a lot of questions about both of you. I called your mom and she told me that you were in the hospital. She said that Tim had assaulted you."

"He did more then assault me, he killed my baby too." The good feeling that I had this morning with Alex faded and the dark sadness returned.

"Oh God Isabella. I didn't know. I didn't know you were pregnant."

"I know that. That's because we aren't friends anymore so you wouldn't know that."

"Don't say that. We are friends. We have been friends for a long time."

"No! No we are not. Friends don't keep secrets, friends don't lose touch because they are sleeping with someone, and friends know when the other one is in trouble. So tell me Tammy, did you know about the drugs too?"

She didn't answer. So, I thought to myself, she knew about that too. My God, what kind of a person has she become?

"Tammy, please leave. I cannot forgive you. I don't trust you, heck, I don't even like you at this point."

A single tear rolled down her face and then she turned and walked out.

A few minutes later Alex walked in with our coffees. He stopped as soon as he saw my face. "What's wrong? What happened? I knew I shouldn't have left."

"It's fine Alex. Tammy came by. I asked her to leave. I told her we were no longer friends."

"Why aren't you friends?"

"She ignored me when she started dating Mike. Mike is friends with Tim. She knew about the affair, and I think she knew something about the drugs too and she never told me. That is not a friend."

"Does she know where he is? How did she know where to find you?"

"She found out where I was from my mom. She heard that something bad happened after Tim didn't show for work."

"Is she on your list for Officer Green?"

"Yep."

As we drank our coffee, he made some calls.

Dr. Young came in. Alex hung up the phone. "How are you feeling today Isabella?"

"Good. When can I leave?"

"I think we can release you today. Your bleeding has almost stopped and like I said yesterday your neck is fine, and there are no other internal injuries. You need to rest for another couple of days. No sexual intercourse for two weeks and follow up with your OB/GYN in two weeks. Do you have any questions?"

I felt embarrassed asking this in front of Alex but I had to know. "Will I still be able to have children in the future?"

"Yes, there is no reason that you shouldn't be able to conceive a child in the future."

"Thank you."

"I will get your discharge paperwork done and then you can leave."

"Thank you."

"I can take you home." Alex stated. "We will get your restraining order first though."

"Okay, let me call my mom and tell her."

Chapter 26

Three hours later we were headed downtown. Alex had already spoken to the judge and everything was ready when we got there. I talked to the judge and explained what happened. The order was granted and then we were on our way to my parent's house.

My mom had prepared my room. It was like I had never left. She had unpacked the suitcases and boxes and set everything back up the way it once was. My mom had made lunch and invited Alex to stay. He accepted and we sat in the kitchen. My dad and Alex talked football while

my mom and I listened patiently. When we were done

eating and visiting, Alex and I curled up on the couch and

watched a movie.

"I should go." He whispered in my ear when the

movie ended. I rested my head back on his chest and

sighed. I didn't want him to go. I liked him with me.

"When will you be back?"

"I will call you tomorrow."

That wasn't what I wanted to hear. I wanted to see

him not talk on the phone but I would take what I could get.

"Okay." I felt sad again but I understood. He kissed my

head and got up. He found my mom and dad in the living

room and thanked them for lunch. I walked him to the door and he turned to me again. "Where's your phone?"

I went to my room and got it and handed it to him. He punched in his number and address in my contacts list. "If you need anything, you call me okay?"

"Okay, I will."

"Don't go out alone until we find Tim. Promise me."

"I promise."

He hugged me and then turned and left. I called Jody to tell her that I was home. She didn't answer so I left her a message. I went to my room and started thinking about what would come next. What will happen when they find Tim? I laid down and rested already missing Alex.

The rest of the weekend was restful and peaceful. I started reading a book and watched movies with my mom and dad. Alex called me twice a day to check on my status. I was hoping that he would come back to see me. I missed spending time with him.

It was getting close to Christmas and I hadn't done any shopping. I was feeling better everyday and with school out on break I had time to get my shopping done. I called Jody to see if she would go with me sometime during the week. I had promised to not go out alone and I wasn't going to tempt fate. We decided to go on Thursday.

I was looking forward to getting out of the house and

started making a list of people that I needed to buy for. I

was planning on going back to work on Saturday night. The

bruising on my neck should be faded enough by then and

the bleeding had stopped. I would be fine.

Thursday morning Jody came by and picked me up.

We headed to the Tucson Mall. It was decorated beautifully

for the holidays complete with a huge tree in the center of

the mall that hosted Santa Clause. It was nice being there

during the week because it wasn't so crowded. We walked

around and picked out gifts for our parents. I secretly

bought a gift for Jody that I told her I was buying for

myself. It was a red silk scarf that I knew would look great

on her. She was desperately looking for something for

Mitchell and I was secretly trying to find something for

Alex. What do you get for a DEA agent slash x-ray tech?

We went into a jewelry shop and I found a silver money

clip that I thought Alex would like. I was lucky that they

did engraving on sight and they placed an ornate '*A*' on the

front of it. I hoped that he liked it. Jody bought Mitchell a

gold chain. It wasn't the mammoth ridiculousness that Alex

wore but it would look great on Mitchell. I was glad that

Jody wasn't the type of person who would pass judgment

on me for buying a gift for Alex after just getting out of a

relationship. She liked the gift I bought for Alex and didn't criticize or ask why I had bought him a gift. We went to

lunch and then headed back to my house. She dropped me

off in front of my house and I gave her hug and told her

that I would see her Saturday night at Patty's. She drove

away as I unlocked the door. My parents were still at work

and I was thinking about all of the great gifts that I scored

today. My mom and I were going to put up the tree this

weekend and I would have all of my gifts wrapped and

ready to put under it. I walked in and locked the door

behind me. I wonder what Alex is doing today? I will call

him tonight if I don't hear from him. I would for sure see

him at Patty's and I couldn't wait. I walked to my room and

set down my purse and my packages. I decided to go to the

kitchen to get a soda. When I walked into the kitchen I froze. I stood staring at the kitchen table and I could hear my own heart beating once again. On the table was a note and a CD leaning up against a red rose in a glass vase. The note had my name on the envelope. I felt for my phone in my pocket as I approached the note. My hand was shaking as I slowly picked it up and opened it. I pulled out a card that had a red rose on the front of it and I opened it.

I know that you really love him. You never loved me, not like I loved you. I will never let him have you. You are mine.

My hand was shaking so hard I almost dropped the card. I didn't know if he was still in the house. I didn't know how he got in. Did he hurt my family? Do I call 911? Do I call Alex? Should I just run first? Wonder if he comes up behind me again? I was in full panic. I pulled out my phone and dialed Alex. He picked up in one ring.

"Hey Isa."

"Alex! I don't know if he is in the house! I don't know if he is here!"

"Isa where are you?"

"My house! Do I run? Alex, oh my God he has been here." I am hyperventilating now.

"Stay on the phone with me Isa. Don't hang up." I heard him on another phone. "Get a car out to 4225 Stonebrook Drive, now! Suspect possibly in the residence, possibly armed and dangerous."

"Isa, are you with me?"

"Yes." I said in a whisper still having trouble breathing. "What do I do Alex? Do I get out of the house?"

"What do you see Isa?"

"There's a note and CD on the table leaning up against a red rose in a vase on the table. I opened the note, it's a card that says,' *I know that you really love him. You never loved me, not like I loved you. I will never let him have you. You are mine.*'

Alex squeezed his eyes closed. Shit, he has been watching us. "What's on the CD?"

"I don't know." I am crying again. "I am too scared to take it to a CD player and I don't want to listen to it alone."

"Isa, a squad car is on the way and so am I."

"Okay."

"I am not going to let anything happen to you."

"Okay."

"Stay in the house until you hear the police there."

"Okay. Alex?"

"Yeah."

"I am scared." I whispered.

"I know. Be tough. I will be there soon."

It was only a minute more and I could hear sirens. "Alex I hear sirens. Do I go outside?"

"Walk over to the door and stay on the phone with me. I am almost there."

I ran to the door and threw it open and ran out knowing they were close. They came up in front of the house and killed the siren. Alex was right, he was right behind them. Officers ran into the house and another one grabbed me and led me behind the car. Alex got out and ran to me. He wrapped his burly arms around me and then looked down at me. "Are you alright?"

I nodded that I was fine. An officer came out and called it all clear. Alex led me back into the house. I showed them what I found on the table and gave another statement to one of the officers. A police officer put on gloves and put the CD in a player. It was just a bunch of songs. Love songs about loss and regret. I looked at Alex still scared. There was no sign of forced entry so how did he get in?

Alex stepped aside and talked with officers for a while. I called my mom and told her what happened. Police suggested that we change all of the locks assuming that he had made a copy of my keys at some point. Police also wanted to know who I thought he was talking about in the note. Who does Tim think I am in love with? I think he is

talking about Alex since he is the only one that I have spent

time with. I didn't know what to say not wanting to get

Alex into any trouble. Alex is the one who gave his input.

"He is talking about me since I stayed with Isa in

the hospital and brought her home when she was

discharged."

"Do you have a romantic relationship with the

victim?"

"No sir." Alex answered.

"What unit do you work for and what is your badge

number?"

Alex complied with the questions. "DEA, badge 1313." I went and got a glass of water and sat down trying to come to terms with what had happened today. Alex was talking to officers in the other room. What was Tim after? Why was he stalking me? The baby was out of the picture and we were through. Why was he doing this? Had he gone crazy?

When Alex came into the room he sat down next to me. I think you should stay with me for a while.

I looked at him stunned. "What? Stay with you knowing that Tim is watching me? He will go berserk."

"I can keep you safe. I can have Terry stay there too if you would feel better."

"My parents are going to flip if I tell them I am going to stay with you."

"It is for your safety Isabella. I will talk to them."

My heart sank a little bit. I know that it is for my safety but a part of me was hoping that he just wanted me with him.

The police left and Alex and I stayed at the house waiting for my parents to come home. I went to my room and packed a bag. I assumed that this would only be for a couple of days. I looked up and Alex was standing in the doorway leaning up against one side of it. He looked serious as I tried to figure out what I needed to bring with me. I stopped and looked over at him tipping my head to the side wondering what he was thinking about. My heart

beats faster just looking at him. I don't know how I am

going to cohabitate with him, even if it is for a short period

of time. I walked over to him still staring him in the eye

and stopped in front of him. "What are you thinking?" I

asked him. Being this close to him is magnetic for me. It is

actually hard for me to keep from reaching out and

touching him. I feel complete and utter lust when I am with

him. I have never felt this way around anyone and it is

unnerving. I am not very sexual but it is all I can think

about when I look at him.

He continued to stare at me and I thought that I

might just orgasm while looking at him as graphic thoughts

ran through my mind. His hand came up and grabbed me

behind my head. He pulled me to him and kissed me hard.

His hand was entwined in my hair as he held me to him and

his tongue pressed into my mouth teasing me. I reached for

his hips and pulled him to me. His kiss was intense and I

returned his advances with every bit of excitement. He

pulled his mouth from mine and we were both breathing

heavily, resting our foreheads together we said nothing, we

didn't have to. He hugged me as we settled down and I

wondered if we could be that close for days without ending

up in bed together. Although I want that very badly, now is

not the time. I felt safe in his arms and we stood like that

for a while. My parents came home an hour later and we all

sat at the table and discussed the situation. My dad called a

locksmith to come out and rekey the locks. I could tell that

they looked distraught about me leaving again but Alex

promised that we would come over on the weekend to set

up the Christmas tree and he assured them that I was safest

with him. We ate dinner with them and then headed out to

go to Alex's house. Alex called Terry on the way. I could

tell that Terry didn't think it was a good idea to take me to

his house. He got off of the phone and I asked him, "Why

doesn't Terry want me to stay with you?"

He looked at me surprised that I had figured that

out.

"I could tell by the way you were answering him." I qualified.

"It isn't protocol to bring a case in close to your home."

"Will this get you into trouble? I can find someone to stay with, I would understand."

He reached over and took my hand and pulled it to his lips. "You are not just a case to me. I care about you and I take care of the people I care about."

I smiled and looked at his profile as we drove. I saw him grin too and it warmed my heart.

We pulled into a gated community in the foothills of Tucson. It was amazing. The houses were secluded and elegant. We pulled into his driveway and then pulled into

the four-car garage. Of course every spot had a vehicle in

it. We were in the truck. I looked over to see what else he

had in here. There was a Porsche, a five series BMW and a

Hummer. But of course, every man's dream, a full

compliment of vehicles. I got out and grabbed my bag. He

walked around and grabbed my hand leading me to the

door leading to the house. We entered the laundry room,

turned off the alarm, and then into a hallway. He turned on

lights as he showed me every room along the way. The

kitchen was gourmet with Viking appliances, granite

countertops and knotty alder cherry colored cabinetry. It

was breath taking. I would be afraid to actually cook in it.

There was a music room with dark leather furniture, a

fireplace and a grand piano in the corner near a window

that overlooked the city. The living room has a plasma TV

mounted on the wall and a softer, more comforting leather

couch and chair. He then showed me where I would be

staying. I was disappointed that he wasn't concerned

enough for my safety that he would want me to be in his

room. After all we have technically slept together once

already. He showed me the other two guest rooms, the

library and his room. His room was breath taking. It had

large, dark, ornate wood furniture with a matching armoire.

There were French doors that led out to the patio and to the

pool and hot tub. The bathroom off of his room looked like

it was designed out of a resort magazine. It had a glass shower with dual showerheads. There was a whirlpool tub, double granite vanity, and another room for the toilet. The walk in closet that was off of the bathroom was the size of my bedroom at home.

"Your home is really beautiful Alex. You did a good job."

"I can't really take credit, my sister designed and decorated it. I just paid for it."

"Is she an architect or a designer?"

"She's a bossy designer."

"I see. Well she has exquisite taste."

"She would agree with you, believe me. Come on the tour isn't done."

"There's more?"

"Just a little bit." I followed him into the closet. Why would we be going into the closet? He pushed his clothes to the side and there was a keypad and a door. He punched in a code and opened the door. "This is a panic room. Do you know what that is?"

"Yes. Why do you have a panic room?"

"I am a DEA agent. It isn't outside the box that some people want to kill me. The code is 2073."

"Got it."

We walked out and he secured his hidden room.

"Want to shoot pool?"

"I didn't see a pool table."

"The game room is on the other side of the family room. Come on."

He was like a kid at a sleep over party. He led me back through the house to the game room. He set up the table and then set up the cue ball to break. I stink at pool, which became very apparent very quickly. He started coaching me, which was a delight. He would lean over behind me and help me line up my next shot. Why would I want to get any better when I can have him leaning up against me? We played a couple of times and then retreated to the living room to watch a movie. I was getting tired by

the time the movie ended.

"I should go get ready for bed." I said as I stood up.

"Good night Alex." I said as I leaned over and kissed his

cheek, got up and started walking toward my room.

He was frowning at me again as he watched me

walk away. He didn't stop me liked I hoped he would.

Chapter 27

I slept better then I had in weeks. I got up and heard voices as I approached the kitchen. I could smell coffee and bacon as I followed the sound of the voices. I rounded the corner and saw Terry sitting at the table drinking coffee and eating breakfast with Alex. They both turned when I walked in.

"Good morning guys."

"Good morning." They both said in unison. Alex got up and poured me some coffee. He handed me a plate and put bacon and eggs on it. I took a seat at the table and started eating. They both were quiet now.

"What did I interrupt?" I asked.

"Terry is going to stay with you tonight while I am at work."

"Okay, but why are you worried about me here?"

They looked at each other. "Isa, we think Tim has connections to some bigger fish in the drug world. He now owes them money because of the drugs he lost, or rather that you threw at him, and he isn't working because he has a warrant out for his arrest for assaulting you. You are his enemy right now. If he depicts you as someone who now has stolen from him, it could be perceived that you now owe the dealer."

I suddenly didn't feel hungry anymore. A drug dealer could be after me? This just won't end will it? "What do we do?"

"Terry and I do our jobs and figure out who his boss is. We get two for one."

"Any idea who he deals with?" Why did I ask this? It wouldn't mean anything to me even if they did know.

"We have a couple of ideas but it's going to take a little time to be sure."

I looked down at my plate trying to regain my composure. A hand came under my chin and gently pulled it up. I was now staring Alex in the eye. I could feel his breath on me and I relaxed and soon as his stare penetrated my thoughts. "Listen to me Isabella. You wouldn't be here if I didn't care about what happens to you. Do you trust me?"

"Yes." My voice was soft and almost a whisper when I answered.

He was still looking at me only inches from my face. I kept staring and I wished Terry wasn't sitting there staring at us because right now I just want to kiss him, among other things, but I would start by kissing him. I then heard Terry clear his throat. Apparently he was afraid that he would have to witness what I was thinking. "I should go shower." I said softly.

Alex nodded at me and let go of my chin. I slid out of my seat and walked back to my room to gather my things.

"Alex, you are too close to this. Having her here is not protocol. It could get you killed. We can arrange a safe house for her."

"I am not officially on this case so I am not breaking protocol."

Terry didn't say anything else he just stared at Alex.

"Terry I know that things just ended with Susana, and I know that Isa's life is a mess right now, but ever since the first day I saw her I have wanted her. I don't know what it is."

Terry continued to sit and listen. "Are you sure she had no involvement in the drugs?"

"No way. I ran a background on her as soon as I found out her name. She is clean. I have watched her before now and she has no involvement. That fucker that she lived with though is in this deep. I am not sure he even intended for it to go this far. He is an amateur and not moving large quantities, but now he has lost a few thousand dollars worth. I think this is new for him. Probably got low on money and parties a little bit. You know how this story goes. They dangle a carrot and some take it and some don't. He is getting desperate now though and he will lash out. It's coming."

Terry sighed signifying he was giving in. "What do we have so far?"

"The word I am getting from my sources says that Fat Frank out of Hermosillo sent a test load up through the Tucson airport. The drop got missed and then the bag went missing. I would guess that Tim opened the bag, realized that nobody would make a claim on the bag and took it for himself. Nobody had heard of Tim Tovar in the bigger circles, which is why I think he is new at this. My snitch says that the word on the street is that this guy sold to small street dealers in order to make some money and dump the load. The problem is Fat Frank owns these dealers. Word got back and Frank sent his boys. Tim now owed Frank and since he didn't have the cash he would have to work it off

for Frank or suffer the consequences. Isa accidentally finds

a small drop that he is supposed to do for one of Franks

goons, probably no bigger than a eight ball, dumps it and

now he is in more shit with Frank. He panics and runs. He

needs money and to stay out of jail. He tries to sweet talk

Isa with the music and flowers. He is mad because he has

seen her with me. He wants her to pay for what she did.

Franks boys are going to pinch him when they get their

hands on him, unless, he produces her to them and portrays

that she took the drugs and now owes Frank because of it."

"What do you think his next move is?"

"I think he is stalking her right now. She is the cause of his problems."

"Do we make a move to shake him up, or bring him in?"

"I think we should bring him in." Alex said after a short consideration.

"If we do that we won't get Frank."

"Frank is untouchable anyway. He never leaves Mexico. The agency just fucks with him by snagging his goons and two bit thugs to slow down his operations. Our only success is to get information that hits a big load coming in. Tim Tovar is not going to have access to that information."

"How do you want to bring him in?"

"I think we should go dancing."

"Dancing." Terry sounded annoyed. "That's the plan?"

"Downtown."

"You are going to use Isa as bait?"

"I am not using her. He is stalking her and assaulted her, remember? But yes, she will bait him in."

"I don't mean to be a sap here but she is working tonight and next weekend is Christmas. What kind of timing did you have in mind?"

"I haven't worked that out yet."

"Are you going to be able to hide her through the holidays?"

"New Years."

"What?"

"We go out on New Years." Alex repeated.

"Alright, New Years it is."

Chapter 28

After I showered and changed I called my parents to see how they were doing. They were going to put up the Christmas tree today. I had decided not to join them. I was sad that I wasn't there but I didn't want to bring danger to them. Alex said that we would go over on Christmas so I could spend time with them. Why doesn't Alex have a tree? I bet his sister could put up a designer tree in the front window that would rival Macy's, I laughed to myself. I walked back out to the family room and the boys were watching sports and lying around. I sat down next to Alex.

"When are you putting up a Christmas tree?"

Alex looked at me with a puzzled look on his face. I heard Terry snicker. "I don't put up a tree."

"Why? Don't you celebrate Christmas?"

"Yes, but it is usually just me here and I don't care to put one up for just myself."

"Can we put one up today?"

"Seriously? It means that much to you?"

"Well, I was thinking about asking your sister to help me design something for the front window."

"Stop. She is not coming here to put up a Christmas tree. It will cost me a fortune and I won't be able to get rid of her."

"Ah, come on Alex." Terry said laughing. "I like it when your sister is here." He winked.

"You stay away from my sister. She will run you into the poor house. Trust me."

"Let's see here," Terry said as he scrolled through his phone, "I have her number right here."

"You have my sister's phone number? Are you kidding me?"

"Alex, she is a very attractive woman. Why would I not capitalize on that?"

"How long have you been hooking up with my sister? Why didn't I know about this?"

"Because of the way you are acting right now." He pushed send on his phone. "Hey baby what 'cha doin'?"

I looked at Alex in total shock. I had no idea when I suggested that his sister come and help us put up a tree that Terry had been connecting with her. Alex looked seriously annoyed now.

"Hey I am at Alex's and him and his new girlfriend are going to put up a Christmas tree today. Want to join us? Her name is Isabella. I don't know ask him. Well, he has to work tonight so how about tomorrow. Oh good, yeah that will help. Why don't you come by my house first and I will bring you over. Yeah, let's say ten. Ciaos baby." Terry hung up the phone. "She needs to buy the decorations today and we will pick up the tree and decorate tomorrow. We

will be here around lunch time to go get the tree."

"I thought you said ten?" Alex replied dryly.

Terry just winked at him. "She's meeting ME at ten.

We'll be here around lunch time."

Alex just rolled his eyes and focused back on the

TV.

"What's your sister's name?" I asked.

Terry answered for him. "Elena, sweet beautiful

Elena, with big brown eyes and long flowing hair and…"

"That's enough Terry."

Terry just laughed but he did stop before it got more

detailed. My hands got sweaty when Terry had declared me

Alex's new girlfriend. I liked the sound of it, but I wasn't

prepared to be introduced into Alex's family as his

girlfriend. What will they think with me staying here and so

soon after Susana? I turned my attention to the TV as well.

College football was not my favorite. Maybe I should go

read my book or call Jody. Just as I was about to get up

Alex took my arm and pulled me down on the couch next

to him. We lay together with me in front of him. It felt

good to be held by him. His arms were wrapped around me

and I entwined my arms in his. Terry didn't seem phased at

all and frankly looked quite at home. I wonder how much

time he typically spends over here?

Before I knew it, it was time to get ready for work.

It would be good to start getting back into my routine. I

went to my room and got changed. Terry was going to

hang out at the bar with me for my entire shift. Alex would

show up after his shift ended. Terry was going to be

seriously bored by the end of the night. They were usually

only there a couple of hours, not seven hours.

We walked into Patty's together. Jody came up and

gave me a hug. Michelle even hugged me and welcomed

me back. I got ready and headed to my section. Nothing

had changed and it was refreshing. Michelle took care of

Terry in the usual corner. It was busy with the regulars as

always. I felt a little nervous wondering if Tim would dare

to come in here. Would he make a scene or wait for us as
we left? I kept looking at the door every time it opened. I
was jumpy, no question. I was filling an order at the bar
when I felt those big familiar hands slip around my waist.
He put his lips close to my ear as I leaned my head slightly
to the side to give him all the room he need in the crook of
my neck. "Don't worry, nothings going to happen to you.
We've got your back."

I hadn't noticed Alex come in. Was it that late
already? A smile slid across my face and I simply said,
"Okay."

He pecked a kiss on my neck and went to the Alex
corner, as I like to call it. Pete set my drink order on the bar

and I placed them on my tray. I could see him looking at

me, waiting for an explanation that I wasn't going to give.

"You here with Alex tonight young lady?"

I don't know why I didn't expect Pete's abruptness.

"I am here working tonight."

He just kept looking at me. What was his concern

with Alex? I took my tray and left without saying another

word.

The night finally came to a close without any

drama. We closed up and all walked out together. Terry

followed us out of the parking lot. He stayed behind us

until we were almost home. "Does Terry live near you?"

"Pretty close. Why?"

"I just noticed that he stayed behind us most of the way home."

"He stayed behind us for security, but yes he doesn't live far."

We pulled into the garage and I followed Alex inside as he disarmed the alarm and turned on the lights. I wondered how long Alex was going to let me stay here. Wonder what if they never caught Tim? I was deep in thought as I started walking toward my room.

"Turning in for the night?" I heard Alex ask.

I turned and smiled. "Yeah. I am beet. How about you?"

He grinned at me and came over and wrapped his arms around me and kissed the top of my head. "Yeah I am tired too."

I had my arms around his waist and was resting my head on his chest. I felt something bulky and in my way and grabbed his shirt and lifted it. "What are you doing?" He asked me laughing.

"You have a gun! Why?"

"In case I need to shoot someone. Why else would I where a gun?"

My face went white. "In case you have to shoot Tim." I stated plainly.

"Maybe but he isn't the only person I am worried about at this point."

"How bad is this Alex?"

He pulled his shirt down and held both of my hands. "I am not sure yet but I think Tim may have gotten involved with a very dangerous drug dealer. Those kind of people mean business."

I thought about this for a moment. "Will they think I know something? Will they come after me too?"

"I don't know Isa, but I am not going to take any chances."

I gave a heavy sigh as I thought about all of this.

"You better get some rest. You will need it after meeting my sister. It will serve you right though since your request for a Christmas tree is prompting her visit." He laughed as he walked over to the refrigerator and grabbed a beer. I walked in behind him and sat down on the bar stool at the counter. He took a long drink from it and set it down on the counter and leaned on the counter across from me. I grabbed the beer and took a drink from it and set it back down. He continued to look at me with those mysterious eyes. I think my breathing was already heavy just looking at him. The thoughts I was having about him were definitely not lady like. He picked the beer back up and finished it. Just like that, two drinks and it was gone. "Let's go." He held out his hand and walked me to my room.

"Good night." He said and gave me a soft kiss on the lips,

and then nipped my ear, and kissed my neck. I groaned

hoping he wouldn't stop, but he did. He rested his head on

my shoulder. I closed my eyes trying to regain my

composure. He lifted his head kissed me lightly again and

left. I turned and walked into my room trying to keep

myself from storming into his room and forcing myself on

him. I fell asleep wondering what it would be like to be

held by him every night and to be with him everyday. It

was so easy to be with him. This is what it is like to love

someone, I thought. It hurts to be away from him and I am

happy to just be in the room with him. It is easy and

comfortable. This is what people talk about and what I hadn't understood before, because I have never felt like this before. Not a minute goes by that I am not thinking about him. Wonder if he doesn't feel the same way about me? Maybe this fiasco with Tim has tainted me in his eyes. I was sad just considering the possibility that he didn't love me back.

Chapter 29

The next morning it was just Alex and me. I was

nervous to come out of my room after deciding last night

that I was in love with him. He would see right through me

I just knew it. I showered and got dressed and felt more

confident about coming out of my room. Alex looked hot

as always in his jeans and a button up shirt with the sleeves

rolled up. I imagine he was hiding his gun under there

again. I smiled as I walked out to the living room. "Good

morning." I was in my favorite jeans and a solid black

fitted t-shirt with a red and black scarf draped around my

neck. I had left my hair down and took time to organize my curls into big flowing waves.

He looked up from reading on his ipad and smiled. "Good morning. Do you want some coffee?"

"Coffee would be great."

He started to get up and I stopped him. "I can get it." I walked into the kitchen and made my coffee and returned to the living room. "Alex?"

"Yeah?" he said as he looked up again.

"I have a favor to ask."

"What is it?"

"I need a ride tomorrow to the doctor's office."

"Of course. Is everything okay?"

"Oh yes, it's just my follow up visit. We didn't bring my car over here with me so I can't take myself. Unless of course you wouldn't mind lending me the keys to the Porsche."

"That is very funny. No, you cannot take the Porsche, and your car is not here for many reasons so don't hesitate to ask when you need to go somewhere."

I thought about that for a few minutes. "What are the reasons that my car isn't here?"

"One, that car is a disgrace to cars and won't look right in my driveway. Two, I don't want you being tracked to this house. I am trying to keep you safe not put a beacon out front that says come and get me."

My mouth was open in utter shock. "A disgrace to cars? Wouldn't look right in your driveway? What is wrong with my car?" I asked with a challenge in my voice.

"What is right with that car?" He shot back.

"You sir, are a snob."

"When it comes to cars that would be true."

"I can't believe you."

He was smiling; loving the fact that he had worked me up so easily. "Well believe it missy."

"Missy? Did you just call me missy? Have you mistaken me for some other woman? My name would be Isabella, not Missy."

He stood up to meet my challenge. He walked up to me and was only inches from my face. "Oh no, I wouldn't mistaken you young lady."

"Really. How so Mr. Snob?"

He took my coffee cup out of my hand and set it on the side table near the couch. He never took his eyes off of mine. "Because every time I look at you all I want to do is take your clothes off and have my way with you."

"Really, I doubt that, in fact I doubt that I am good enough for you at all."

"You question?"

"I don't question, I know. I bet I am just another Mustang in this house, huh?"

"Oh you have no idea young lady." He grabbed me around the waist and pulled me to him kissing me hard. There was longing in this kiss and I could feel it. I wanted it and I returned that need teasing him with my tongue, doing everything I could to draw him into me. I let my hands drop down and rubbed him feeling his erection through his jeans. I was going for this. I was not letting this go, I wanted him and I wanted him to know it. His hand was behind my head and his other one grabbed me from behind and pulled me in closer. I rubbed him harder letting him know that I wanted him. I pulled on his jeans and unbuttoned them. I pulled the zipper down and slid my hand in. Oh my god, he feels too good. I wrapped my hand around him and start stroking him. He picked me straight

up and carried me to his room. He laid me down on the bed

and came down on top of me. His hand unbuttoned my

jeans and zipper without effort while still kissing me. He

grabbed my shirt and pulled it over my head taking the

scarf with it. I was breathing so hard I thought I would

hyperventilate with wanting him. He looked down at me.

"You are so beautiful Isa." He slowed down and started

kissing my neck, moving down to my breasts. He kissed me

through me bra and his hand pushed down my jeans. I was

just in my bra and underwear as he continued to tease me

through my bra and his hand trailed down my belly. I

arched up wanting him. I started unbuttoning his shirt and

pushed it off of him. Shit he has his gun on. How do I get

that off? He reached around and pulled off the holster and

gun and put them on the nightstand never stopping his

torment with his hands. I reached down and pulled down on

his jeans. I wanted to see him and feel him. I ran my hands

over his chest and he groaned at my touch. He undid my

bra while kissing me and pushed it to the side landing his

lips on my nipple. I yelled out wanting more and his hand

pulled on my other nipple. He was grinding his erection on

me and it felt so good. I just wanted him in me and returned

his movements by pushing my hips into him. I slid my

hands down into his boxers and squeezed his cheeks,

rubbing them and pushing him closer into me. His hand

pushed my underwear to the side and his fingers found me

wet and wanting him. He gently circled my clitoris and I

was shaking trying not to lose control already. He didn't

stop though, he kept touching me and circling me as I

groaned and gasped. His finger entered into me but he

continued to stroke me and I came. Arching and screaming

I came hard. He didn't stop he kept it coming and then he

put his mouth back on my nipple and didn't let me come

down from my high. He reached up and pulled the

nightstand open pulling out a condom. He ripped it open

with his teeth. I pushed his boxers completely off and he

rolled the condom on. He got between my legs and lifted

both of my legs over his shoulders. I was scared at how

large this man was. For a split second I was worried that

this would hurt. That was until his mouth came down on

me and I was lost in delight once again as his tongue

readied me to come again. He sucked and kissed me and I

felt his tongue in me. I was screaming now wanting him

badly. He then leaned up and entered into me gently. Oh,

he felt so good, he completely filled me and I was

rhythmically moving against him wanting this feeling to

not stop. "You are so tight baby. You feel so good around

me." He was matching my movements and then he took

over moving faster back and forth and then harder, and

faster. I was screaming, wanting this, wanting all of this

and then I couldn't take any more I was coming, coming so

hard and then I heard him too. We came together so hard as we both groaned and grabbed each other not wanting it to end. We laid there together trying to catch our breath. He was still inside me and his head was next to mine on the pillow. "Isabella?"

"Yeah?"

"I hope I didn't just scare you away?"

"Did I give you the impression that I was running away?"

He smiled and kissed my neck. "Good because that was amazing."

"You're not kidding."

We fell asleep in each other's arms and didn't wake
until we heard the doorbell. We both jumped up looking
around disoriented. I looked at the clock. It was noon
already. We've been asleep all this time. I laughed as we
stumbled around the room looking for our clothes and
hurrying to get dressed. The doorbell rang again and then a
knock on the door. Alex flung the condom into the
bathroom garbage can and we both continued to pull on
clothes and straighten up trying to not let our secret become
obvious. Alex's phone started to buzz and he grabbed it.
"Yeah." He listened, "I'm coming, I'm coming. Just relax
Elena." He grabbed my hand and threw his phone down on
the bed as we walked toward the front door. Just before he

opened it he turned to me and smiled and leaned down and

kissed me, cupping my face in his hands. "Ready for this?"

My eyes were wide with anticipation. "I guess so." I

smiled back.

There was a pounding on the door and then Alex

threw the door open. "Hold your horses. I was coming."

Looking back at Alex was one of the most exotic

women I have ever seen. She had long, brown, wavy hair,

thin, tall, oval brown eyes and flawless skin. She was

wearing black boots with her jeans tucked in, a cashmere

sweater, large hoop earings, a thick gold chain that matched

Alex's, and gold bracelets. She came walking in and

hugged Alex, kissing him on the cheek. "Como esta. Que estas haciendo aqui?" She was grinning at him.

He kissed and hugged her back and ignored her question. "Elena this is Isabella. Isabella this is my sister Elena."

I held out my hand, "It's nice to meet you."

She shook it back and smiled slightly, "It's nice to meet you to." She looked back at Alex and said, "Una chica blanca, Alejandro?"

Alex rolled his eyes and said, "Knock it off or this will be the shortest visit you've ever had here."

Terry came in and shook Alex's hand and then hugged me. "How are you doing Isabella?" he said quietly to me.

"Fine thanks." I smiled warmly at him.

Elena chimed in. "Well, I have gathered some of the most beautiful decorations that Scottsdale has to offer. It is a good thing that you called me when you did. I never would have been able to do all of this in just one afternoon." She looked around. "Where's the tree?"

"We were waiting for you." Alex said flatly. "And I thought it would take you longer to get here." He looked at Terry.

"Why would it have taken me longer? Terry knows what I like and never keeps me hanging." She was being coy with him and I enjoyed the banter between these two. "Let's get going." She started walking toward the door and Terry followed.

Alex grabbed his keys and we went out to his Hummer. We pulled out of the driveway and followed Terry and Elena. "Are you okay? She can be a real pill."

"I am fine." I grinned as I said this. I get the feeling that his sister doesn't really like any woman that is with her brother.

We went to a local tree lot, but Elena didn't like any of the trees. We visited a second lot and she didn't like those either. "Alejandro, we need to get an artificial tree. These trees are basura."

"Fine, whatever, let's just pick something already."

I could tell that he was getting annoyed but she didn't seem to notice, or she just didn't care. She finally picked a tree at one of the mall's high-end department stores. We brought it home and then she directed where it would be put up. It was entertaining watching Terry and Alex struggle with assembling the ten foot, Fraser Fir look alike. Once it was up Elena went to work. We made several trips back and forth from Terry's SUV to the house, unloading her purchases. She knew exactly how she wanted it to look and directed us all on what to put on the tree and how. When it was finally finished it was breathtakingly

beautiful. It was blue and silver with a silver star on top. I

had to say it looked like in should be in the Macy's

showroom. She stood back and smiled, happy with her

creation.

"What do you think Alejandro?"

He looked at me, "Do you like it?"

Elena looked annoyed that he didn't answer her

question and deferred it to me.

"Oh yes, it's lovely. Thank you for doing this

Elena."

She smiled but didn't say another word.

Alex smiled back at me not meeting her stare.

"It's dinner time and I am starving." Terry broke the awkward silence.

"Me too." Elena said, "What are you making us Alejandro?"

"Gee, here I thought I would get some homemade tacos or even some tamales, but wait, that's right, you don't know how to cook do you?"

"I am not your keeper or your wife Alejandro. I don't need to cook for you, and I can cook."

"Well, knowing that it's the one thing you're not perfect at, I took the liberty of taking out steaks to throw on the grill."

"I can cook." She stated again.

"I'll let mom be the judge of that." Alex was laughing now, enjoying making her mad. He opened a bottle of red wine and poured each of us a glass. He scrubbed potatoes and wrapped them in foil. He walked out and turned on the grill.

"So, do you work with Alejandro?" Elena asked me.

"At the hospital I do." I answered.

"What do you do?"

"I take x-rays."

"How long have you known each other?"

"Since August."

"Where did you meet?"

"At the hospital. How long have you been a designer?" I tried to change the subject.

"For about five years."

"Do you live in Scottsdale?"

"Yes."

"Do you work for a firm or are you independent?"

"Independent contracts."

"What's your specialty?"

"Home design."

"Alex says you designed this house."

"Yes I did." She said flatly not liking the borage of questions that I was throwing back at her.

Alex came back in and Terry looked relieved. We

started talking about the upcoming holidays and what

everyone was doing to celebrate. I wasn't sure what Alex

was doing but I was hoping to spend some time with my

parents. I thought about how pretty soon winter break

would be over and I would need to go back to school. Jody

and I are going to do a rotation on evenings, which will be

good if Tim is still after me. At least Alex and Terry will be

around.

After dinner Terry and Elena decided to go. It takes

at least two hours to get back to Scottsdale and I am sure

she wanted some alone time with Terry first. We walked

them to the door to say our good byes. She shook my hand

and gave her brother a hug and kiss. Terry hugged me and shook Alex's hand. Alex closed the door behind them and turned to me. "Congratulations, you survived Elena Ortiz."

I laughed. "She isn't that bad."

"Yes, she is."

I didn't reply.

"Do you like your tree?"

"It's fabulous. Thank you."

"You're welcome."

Alex was quiet for a few minutes. "What time is your appointment tomorrow?"

"At eleven at the hospital. The clinics are on the eighth floor."

"Want to hot tub for a little while before we call it a night?"

I grinned back at him. "I would love to but I didn't bring a suite. I didn't know you had a pool."

"It doesn't matter because I would just take it off of you anyway."

"Really."

"Really."

"We're skinny dipping?"

"Call it what you want but we won't be needing suites."

"He grabbed our wine glasses and walked out the back door."

He must have turned it on when he was grilling the steaks because it was already hot. We undressed and hurried in. He pulled me close to him and I snuggled up against him. I rested my head on his shoulder and enjoyed the star filled sky. "I'm glad that you are here with me Isa."

"Me too."

He smiled back at me. We relaxed for about an hour just enjoying being together. "Should we call it a night?"

"Okay."

He got up and pulled two towels out of a warmer. I stood up and he wrapped one around me. He dried himself off with the other one and wrapped it around his waist. His body is so perfectly sculpted. I just never get sick of looking at it. He turned off the hot tub and took my hand as

we walked in. He led me to his room with him and my

heart was beating with anticipation. He pulled back the

covers and turned back to me. He kissed me slowly and

pulled me close. I wanted him as much now as I did earlier.

His kiss was sensual and passionate. I get drunk just tasting

him, wanting more. He pulled my towel loose and let it

drop to the floor. I pulled his from around his waist leaving

us both naked. His hands trailed down my body and rested

on my hips. I leaned into him wanting to feel him against

me. Our kiss intensified and I move my hands to cover him,

stroking him gently. I drop down to my knees and take him

in my mouth. Moving slowly I lick him up and down and

then start sucking on him. He groaned and put his fingers in

my hair. I am taking him in deep, sucking on him hard

when he pulls me up to my feet and kisses me again. He

reaches down putting his finger in me and stroking me

making me shake all over. He kisses my neck and my

nipples and I am grasping his shoulders knowing that I

can't hold on much longer. He stops right before I am

going to come and turns me around and leans me over the

bed. He guides me up onto it and I am face down. He is

over me while I am face down and pulls my hips up so I am

on my hands and knees. He reaches down between my legs

again and I am still ready. I want to come now and I hear

him pull the nightstand drawer open and the foil rip. He

enters me slowly and I am amazed at how good this makes

me feel. He is squeezing my bottom as he pushes into me

and I groan with pleasure. His hands are on my hips and he

is moving me with him. Feeling him moving in and out of

me is erotic and I am gripping the sheets ready to explode.

My groans explode into a scream of desire as I feel myself

spasm with desire around him. He grabs me hard and he is

with me as we both climax hard. I lay down on my stomach

with him still with me. We are both trying to catch our

breath. He rolls to the side and takes me with him. He pulls

the sheet over us and we drifted off to sleep. I am so in love

with this man. I want him with me always.

When I woke up in the morning I turned to look at Alex. He was still sleeping and looked so peaceful. He was so handsome and I just liked to look at him. I didn't get to stare long and he opened his eyes. "Good morning." I said quietly as I reached up and ran my hand over his face.

He smiled and turned his face to kiss my hand.

"Good morning."

"How did you sleep?"

"Like a rock. How about you?"

"The same."

"Want breakfast?"

"Coffee is good for me."

"Me too. I'll put some on and I will be right back."

I heard him in the kitchen grinding the coffee and I looked around his room. I wonder if he will let me stay in here every night with him? The room was huge but warm and comfortable. I could stay here all day. He came back in and climbed in next to me. He pulled me to him and kissed me. "I have to work tonight but Terry will hang out with you until I get home." I nodded my head in agreement.

We got up and showered together and went to my appointment. The doctor gave me a clean bill of health and sent me on my way. He renewed my birth control prescription and suggested not going off of it for any reason until I was ready to have children. Thanks for the tip, I thought to myself.

Chapter 30

The week of Christmas went by quickly. I missed hanging out with Jody but we talked on the phone daily and I was looking forward to being back in school and at the hospital in order to see her more. Things were going strong with her and Mitchell and they were talking about getting an apartment together over the summer. I was so happy for her. I wondered if after this mess was cleared up with Tim if Alex would want me to stay. I felt sad thinking about the possibility that he wouldn't want me to live here with him.

I loved him but I knew if I said those words to him it would seem like he was just a rebound for me. I was looking forward to seeing my parents tomorrow on Christmas day. Alex and I are going over in the morning and then in the evening we are having a party here.

Terry is here hanging out with me today because Alex had to work the day shift as his holiday shift. Tonight Alex and I are planning to spend the evening alone and have a quiet dinner together.

"What are you doing tonight Terry? Do you have family in town?"

"No, my family is all in Missouri. Elena is gonna spend this evening with me."

I grinned at him. "Don't worry, your secret is safe with me. Is she coming with you tomorrow night?"

"Yes. She isn't going home to visit her parents until New Years."

"I am surprised. I figured her for a huge New Years partier."

"She is, but I am busy that night so she is going else where."

"What are you busy with?"

"Going out with you and Alex."

"Where are we going?"

"Downtown."

I frowned. "This is business, not pleasure, isn't it?"

"Yes it is. It's time to finish this thing."

"Okay." I said quietly. I was scared. I was scared of Tim, scared of who he was involved with and scared of losing Alex when it was all over.

"It will be okay Isabella. We will take care of you."

I smiled, but with sadness in my eyes. "I know." I paused for a while busying myself with preparing dinner for Alex and me for later. "Does Elena know why I am here?"

"Not really. She thinks you two are just using each other as rebound material."

I thought about that for a minute. That's what I was afraid of. Maybe we are. How will I know if this is real?

Alex came home at about five. Terry hung out and drank a couple of beers with him and I got dinner started. I brought out some shrimp cocktails for all of us and we sat in front of the tree and ate them. I put on Christmas music, which they both complained about, but I protested that it was Christmas Eve and it was tradition for me. Terry left about an hour later after receiving a text message. I assume that Elena was close and he needed to go. After he left I finished cooking our dinner. Alex opened a glass of wine for us and joined me in the kitchen. I felt sad knowing this was probably the last week I had here with him. That after New Years there would be no reason that I needed to stay.

Alex sensed my sadness and put his arms around me.

"What's the matter Isa?"

I didn't want to say what was on my mind. I didn't

want him to know how much I wanted to be with him.

"Nothing."

He turned me around to face him and pulled my

chin up so I was looking him in the eye. "What's the

matter? Talk to me."

I sighed. I guess if I really do love him then I better

learn to trust and communicate with him. "Terry told me

that we are going out on New Years." I paused. "That it

was business not pleasure."

"Go on."

I stood staring at him and my eyes filled with tears. "I was just sad knowing this will come to an end." There I said it. Prepare to have my heart broken when he agrees with me that this will end.

He stood very still and stared into my eyes for a long moment. I was coming out of my skin wondering what he was going to say. "What would come to an end?"

He was going to torcher me. "This. This fairy tail that I get to live with you right now."

"Fairy tale?"

I shook my head in affirmation. "Yes, this amazing life of going to bed with you at night and waking up with you in the morning. Dinners shared together and quiet moments when we don't need to talk because it's so comfortable to just be together. Feeling like I can't walk by you without touching you, and then giving in and touching you and not wanting it to stop. Learning what foods you like and don't like, knowing you are waiting for me after my Saturday shift, and watching football together on Sunday's. I want you to want me. Not because you feel like you have to take care of me but because I want you to want me too." Well that was more then I intended to say but there it was, everything but the three fatal words.

"And what makes you think it will end?"

He isn't going to give me an inch is he? I stayed

quiet, trying to decide what to say next. "Because I will

need to go when you no longer need to protect me."

There, the ball is in his court. He continued to look

down at me. "I don't want to pressure you Isabella."

Here we go, he is going to try to let me down softly.

Why did I have to ruin my own Christmas? "I know." That

was all I could say without crying.

"No, you don't know." He said back at me. "You

don't know that really I want to take you in every room of

this house. You don't know that ever since I laid eyes on

you that you are in my thoughts all of the time. You don't

know that I wanted to kill Tim when I saw you in that

hospital bed. You don't know that I wish it was us that had

made a baby together and didn't have to live through the

pain that we have had to endure. You don't know that I

don't want you to go, that really I fell in love with you

before you even knew my name and I wish I hadn't wasted

so much time with a woman that was poison for me. You

don't know because I was afraid if you did know that you

would run away."

I stood listening to his catharsis that I thought

would be filled with all of the reasons that we couldn't be

together. He said that he loved me. I stared back at him. He

said he loved me, I thought again. I grabbed him by the

neck and pulled him down to me and kissed him. I kissed

him like there wasn't a tomorrow, like I couldn't leave him

ever, like I needed him now. He kissed me back and I was

lost. Lost in the love that I felt for this man. He pulled my

shirt over my head and pulled his off in return. We were

undoing each others pants and in a matter of seconds we

were naked in the kitchen. He lifted me up onto the counter

and continued to caress and kiss me. He started to reach for

his pants to get a condom out. "What's wrong?" I asked.

"Nothing, I just need a condom."

I pulled him back to me. "No you don't Alex. I am

on birth control again. Everything is fine. I am fine. Please

let me feel you."

He looked at me and kissed me again. "Are you

okay with that? You don't have to have unprotected sex

with me."

I looked at him surprised that he was doing this for

me, because he thought that's what I wanted. "Alex, I am

so in love with you. Please, please let me have this."

He kissed me hard and stroked me until I was

panting with desire and then he pulled me toward him and

he slid into me. I was still on the counter but he had me by

the hips pulling me onto him. He felt so good. I groaned

just feeling him enter me. "Oh my god Alex, yes, yes." We

moved in tandem until we both couldn't take anymore and

exploded with desire together. He pulled me off of the

counter never leaving me and walked us to living room. We laid down in front of the tree. He looked down at me with so much desire and love in his eyes. "I love you Isa."

"I love you too."

"I want you to stay with me, please say you will."

I smiled up at him. "I can't afford the rent."

He flipped us around so that I was on top. "Then I will take it in trade."

"Will you now?"

"Oh yeah."

He turned me around and lifted my hips to his mouth. I looked down to see that he was hard again and took him into my mouth. This time he wasn't going to stop me. It was hard to focus with him bringing me to orgasm

yet again with his mouth, but I was successful this time and

he came into my mouth. I turned myself so my head was

back up by his. We collapsed together in front of the tree

holding each other. Food just didn't seem important right

now. Alex kissed my forehead and pulled me close. He

whispered in my ear, "I want to give you your gift tonight."

I smiled, "You can't it's not Christmas yet."

"I have to give it to you tonight. It can't wait."

I looked at him. "Okay, if you insist."

"Get up. I can't wait." He went to the kitchen and

gathered our clothes. What is it that can't wait? "Sit here

and close your eyes."

"I have to close my eyes?"

"Yes. Don't argue. Please."

"Okay, okay. They are closed." I sat there for a long moment wondering where he had run off to. I heard the door open. Where is he going to get my gift. I heard the door open again and he set something in front of me.

"You can open your eyes."

There was a decorative box in front of me with holes in it and a whining sound from within. I pulled the lid off and inside was an English bulldog puppy. It was the cutest puppy that I had ever seen. She just looked up at me and cried. "Oh sweet puppy come here." I said as I lifted her from the box. "Were you scared in there? Oh Alex, she is beautiful. Thank you." I kissed him while holding the

puppy.

"Do you like her?"

"I love her. She is the cutest puppy I have ever

seen."

He smiled at me. "What do you want to name her?"

I thought for several minutes. What would be a

good name for this puppy? "How about Lola?"

"Lola?" He looked at her. "I like it. Lola it is."

Alex pulled me close and put his arm around me

while I held Lola. We couldn't stop looking at her. She

cuddled up in my arms and fell asleep. My heart was over

flowing with happiness. First because I was so happy and

in love with Alex and second because I now have this new

addition to our family. Little Lola makes us a family. We

sat staring at her for what seemed like hours. When she

woke we took her outside and then came in for dinner.

After dinner I gave Alex his gift. It just didn't seem like

enough after everything he has given me but he seemed to

really like the money clip. We played with Lola for a while

and then put her in her new kennel for the night. We went

to bed and curled up together falling asleep entwined in

each other's arms.

I only had to get up once with Lola during the night

but I had to wake up Alex to turn off the house alarm in

order to take her out. We got up in the morning feeling the

effects of interrupted sleep. I couldn't wait to see my parents and to show them Lola. We had our morning coffee and then showered up and got ready for our day.

My mom was so happy to see me when we got there she hugged me for a full minute before I could peel myself out of her arms. Alex was holding Lola and I turned and took her from him in order to show her to my parents. They thought she was the cutest puppy they had ever seen. I helped my mom prepare our turkey lunch and we all sat down together to eat.

"When do you think you will be moving back home?" My mother asked.

I didn't know what to say. She would be so disappointed in me for moving in with another man after what just happened.

Alex could see the turmoil on my face and answered for me. "It is hard to say how long this investigation is going to take, but Isabella is welcome to stay as long as she likes."

My mom didn't say anything; she just looked between the two of us. She knew, I didn't need to say a word.

After dinner we had pie and then retreated to the living room to exchange gifts. My mom had even bought something for Alex. I could see the surprise on his face as he took the gift and began to open it. It was a cigar humidor

and three cigars were wrapped and placed inside of it. He

was grinning ear to ear obviously happy with what he had

received. "Thank you. I love cigars. How did you know?"

My mom smiled back. "I am glad that you like it. I

made a lucky guess."

I had signed the gifts that I had bought for my

parents from Alex and me. I know that my mom took note

of that but my dad didn't seem to notice. They opened their

gifts thanking us and complaining that we had spent too

much. I opened my gift and was shocked to see a ring box.

I opened it a little confused why my parents would buy me

a ring. Then I heard my mom explain. "It was your great

grandmothers engagement ring. I had it restored and now it

is yours. I know how much you love looking at my old

jewelry and I thought that you would like it."

Tears filled my eyes. What a beautiful and

thoughtful gift. "I love it. Thank you so much." I got up

and hugged my mom and my dad. I put the ring on my right

hand. It fit perfectly. I can't remember another Christmas

that was as perfect as this one. We stayed and visited for a

while longer and then headed home to get ready for our

party. We went to work putting ice in the coolers and

preparing food. Alex indulged my need for Christmas

music but made it clear that at the party it was back to top

forty hits. Lola played at my feet as I prepared trays of

appetizers. I watched Alex set up his humidor and smiled at how much he liked the gift my mom had given him. My parents looked very wary when I removed more things from my room to take with me this afternoon. I think they know that Alex and I are more then just friends or a bodyguard. Alex looked up and caught me staring at him with a smile. He came over and planted a passionate kiss on me that made me want to strip him down on the spot. We were making out in the kitchen hot and heavy when the doorbell rang. Alex looked up at the clock as the bell rang again. "It must be Terry and Elena. God forbid she didn't inspect that everything was to her liking before a party." Alex grumbled.

He swung open the door and Elena pushed her way in. "Hello. Merry Christmas." Elena said as she walked in and kissed Alex and kept moving in toward the kitchen. "I am here to help. What needs to be done?"

I smiled calmly at her as she entered the kitchen attempting to take over. "Hi Elena. Merry Christmas."

"Merry Christmas Isabella." She smiled coolly. "I came early to help you and Alejandro prepare for the party."

"Well thank you, that was very thoughtful of you." I looked over at Alex and Terry as they entered the kitchen. Alex grabbed a beer for him and Terry out of the refrigerator and pulled a bottle of wine out to open for

Elena and myself.

"What appetizers have you chosen? How many

people are you expecting?"

"Elena, it is all done. We made prosciutto and

cheese wraps, escargot, there is caviar and crackers, wine,

beer, soda, you name it and we have it."

Elena turned and looked at Alex. "Well done little

brother. You are learning."

"It was Isabella that put it all together." Alex

responded.

Elena didn't say anything and Terry walked up

behind her wrapping an arm around her waste. She didn't

say another word but just looked between the two of us.

Alex grinned at her, which was just making her mad. The

doorbell rang breaking the awkward silence. I was so

grateful to see Jody and Mitchell at the door. I gave Jody a

long hug and they came in to join us. I showed everyone

Lola and I think even Elena melted looking at her. I held

her for a long time as people started filtering in. Before

long the party was buzzing with all of our closest friends.

After a couple of hours I went into the bedroom to put Lola

in her kennel. As I turned to leave the bedroom, I was

startled by Elena standing in the doorway. "Oh! Crap Elena

you scared me. I didn't hear you come in."

Elena looked at me for a long moment with the look of hate in her eyes and then said, "What's going on with you and my brother?" She obviously had had a few drinks in her.

"What do you mean?"

"You know what I mean Isabella. What's going on with you two? Are you a new toy or a case he is working on?"

The question made me mad. A new toy? How rude. "Why don't you ask Alex if you have questions about our relationship?"

"Your relationship? Are you the reason that he is not with Susana anymore? Did you break them up?"

I was flabbergasted. She didn't know why they broke up. "No, I am not the reason that they aren't together."

Elena came up to me as close as she could stand and said, "I don't believe you. I think you wormed your way into my brother's bed and broke them up. Do you know how much she meant to him? How much he loved her?"

I didn't want to envision Alex loving anyone else and the thought brought tears to my eyes. Before I could say a word Alex burst around the corner and into the room.

"What the hell is going on in here Elena?"

She turned around as startled as I was.

"You don't know shit about me and Susana."

"I know that you loved her. I know that you wanted to marry her."

I gasped even though I already knew that he had proposed to her.

"Elena, you don't know what you are talking about and you need to drop it, it's none of your business."

"It is my business if it concerns you and your happiness. Did this girl ruin your relationship with Susana?'

"No, Susana did me a favor and showed me how bad our relationship really was."

"What are you saying Alejandro? You loved her!"

"No Elena! I thought I loved her but that is not what it was. It was a relationship of convenience, nothing more."

"How can you say that after all of the years you had together? You were her first. She gave herself to you."

I did not want to hear this. I did not need to know that he took her virginity.

"Shut up Elena. You don't know what you are talking about."

"I won't shut up Alejandro! I won't be quiet about you throwing away the best thing that has ever happened to you!"

"She is not the best thing that ever happened to me."

"Bullshit! You are blinded by this piece of ass and I am not going to stand for it!"

Piece of ass? That is just not nice.

"Elena, that is enough! Stop it right now."

"NO, NO, I won't stop it!"

"Tell her Alex." I said calmly but firmly. I almost didn't recognize my own voice. "Tell her the truth or she'll never understand."

Alex looked at me. His face had so much pain in it. "It is none of her business Isa."

"Tell me what?" Elena said looking between us.

Alex and I were staring at each other. "She is your family Alex."

He looked at me and I knew he didn't want to confide in her. "I don't need the whole world to know this. It is painful enough."

I walked over to him and wrapped my arms around him. "The whole world doesn't need to know, but your family does. They need to understand what you have been through."

He looked down at me for a long moment. The pain in his eyes was hard to look at. I understood that loss, that emptiness.

"Alejandro, what the hell is she talking about?" Elena burst out in her abrasive way.

Alex never stopped looking at me and I never let go of him as he spoke to her without looking at her.

"Elena, shut up and listen for a minute. I got Susana pregnant."

"Oh my God. You bastard. You left her because she was pregnant?"

He whipped his head around and looked at her. "Shut the fuck up Elena! I would never do that and I would think that you could give me that much credit!"

Elena snapped her mouth closed.

"I took her to Cancun and proposed to her. She took the ring and then told me that I may not want to marry her anymore. When I asked her why she would think that, she said because she had aborted the baby."

Elena gasped. "No, no, she wouldn't."

"Yes. Yes she would, and yes she did. I was devastated Elena. I would have raised that child myself but she didn't give me the decency of even a conversation. She just took the life of my child."

Elena ran to Alex and threw herself at him throwing her arms around his neck pushing me out of the way. Alex pulled her off and looked at her. "My feelings for Isa have nothing to do with Susana. I am just glad that I am not married to that evil woman." He looked at Elena for a moment more. "You owe Isa an apology Elena. I love

Isabella. I really love her. I wish I would have known what this emotion was so I wouldn't have wasted so much time on Susana. Isa is what I want, who makes me happy and who I love. If you can't accept that then you will have to distance yourself from us."

Elena looked at Alex for a long moment. She finally turned to me. "I am sorry Isabella. I am glad that you make my brother so happy. That is all that I want for him."

"I will do everything in my power to make him happy Elena. I love him and want to take care of him."

Her eyes became teary when I said that.

"I hope that you take good care of him always and don't break his heart like it has already been broken."

"Never. I will never hurt him." I said in reply.

Elena turned to Alex and kissed his cheek. "I am going to kill Susana. I am going to kill her for hurting you and for taking a niece or nephew from me. She had no right."

"Let it go Elena. That little spirit will come back to me another time."

I had never heard Alex make a spiritual comment before. It warmed my heart and made me sad at the same time.

She turned and left the room. Alex pulled me to him and kissed me. "I am sorry that my sister attacked you."

"It's okay. At least now she knows the truth and isn't walking around thinking that I was the other woman that broke up you and Susana."

He smiled down at me. "Let's go join our party."

We went back out into the living room and Alex turned up the music. He grabbed me and pulled me close to dance with him. I had danced with him at the club but this was different. There was Latin music playing and he held me close as we spun endlessly to the music. It didn't seem to bother him that I had no idea how to dance to this music. It wasn't long before the majority of people at the party were dancing as well. It was Alex's ipod that was playing so the music changed genre every song but it didn't matter because we just kept dancing.

It was hours before the party ended. I was exhausted but we had a great time. Even Elena had fun dancing and mauling Terry all night. We said good-bye to each of our guests as people began to leave. Alex picked me up and carried me to his room. Being with him was a perfect ending to a perfect holiday.

Chapter 31

As the week went on I became more and more nervous about New Year's Eve. I just wanted Tim to go away. How were we going to catch him? Alex and I practiced shooting every day. He never said that I would have to carry a gun but he definitely wanted me to be able to handle one. Terry was coming over tonight to discuss the plan. I hope whatever it is that it works. I am supposed to start back to school on Monday and I don't want to walk around afraid anymore.

The day was here and Alex had his game face on.

When Terry showed up we started to get ready. They both

vested up and concealed weapons. I don't have a license to

conceal a weapon so I wouldn't be carrying a gun. Alex did

make me wear a vest though. He said that he just wanted to

take every precaution. They were both wired and taped a

wire to me too. The earpieces looked like any other blue

tooth. Nobody would think anything of it. We were heading

downtown where they were having club crawl. One

wristband gets you into all of the downtown clubs and they

each have a different band playing. It was hopping when

we got there. I didn't need to show my ID since Alex knew

the guy selling the wristbands and paid for all of us without question. We started walking and went into the first bar.

Alex ordered beer for him and Terry and water with lime

for me. They didn't really even drink they were just for

show. Alex draped an arm around me while looking and

searching the room. We stayed about an hour and went to

the next bar. This time Terry went off on his own and me

Alex stood up against the bar. Suddenly Alex said

something that was meant for Terry to hear. "Hit man ten

o'clock." He grabbed my arm and we started walking into

the crowd. I didn't know who Alex was talking about even

as I scanned the room trying to not look panicked. Alex

pushed us through the door and out onto the sidewalk. He

never let go of my arm and we were moving fast. We

ducked into the next bar and off to a corner. I had no idea

where Terry was. Then I could here him on my earpiece.

I've got sight of him. That's one of Frank's. Shit, he knows

we are here. The jig is up, retreat now. Alex grabbed my

hand and we hurried out and toward where we entered the

event. We all met up at the car and got in. Nothing more

was said and we drove away quickly. We just drove around

while Alex ensured we weren't being tailed.

"Well, we know he is involved with Frank. It was

intentional that his hit man was visible to us. That was a

warning." Alex said to Terry.

"We need to report back to head quarters. This is a

bigger problem then originally anticipated."

We went back to Alex's and they retreated to the den while I waited. I had no idea what was going on or how we were going to solve it.

When they came out they both looked worried and that scared me. I needed to know what was going on. "How would Frank or his men know who you guys are?"

They looked at each other for a minute. "I know Frank personally." Alex finally said. "I went to school with his little brother. I have advised on cases that involve Frank but I have never taken him on. He doesn't know that I am DEA but he knows that I know what he does for a living and it is implied that I never speak of it. I have been seen with you and you made life uncomfortable for one of his sales men. He is letting me know that I can be eliminated as well as you."

"You read all of that into seeing a supposed hit man for Fat Frank?"

"I have seen it before. I know I am right."

"What do we do now? How do make this stop?"

They didn't answer and that scared me even more. Terry stayed at our house that night. It was the worst New Year's ever, and after having the best Christmas ever. I didn't sleep at all as I worried about the future and how this was going to end.

Chapter 32

Monday I went to class and welcomed some normalcy in my life. It was good to see Jody and we picked up where we left off at the party. Her New Year's brought an engagement ring and I was so happy for her. She was positively glowing. I wondered if someday Alex and I would tie the knot. First we need to end this Tim and Frank business, I thought to myself.

The week wore on and we were off to clinicals on Wednesday. Jody and I were going to get to work from 3 pm to 11 pm on a trauma rotation. I liked it because I was going to get to work with Alex, and Jody was going to get to work with Mitchell too.

The night was going by quickly and I was walking back to the department with Alex after going to the floor for a portable exam. We turned the corner and a man came up to Alex in the hall and shook his hand. "Hey Alejandro. It's been a long time. What are you doing here?"

Alex shook his hand but clearly looked concerned. "Hey Tito. I am good, how are you? What are you doing here?"

"I am here to see my mother. She just had surgery. Are you working here?"

"Yeah, I work here."

They looked at each other for a long time saying

nothing more. "Is your brother here too?" Alex then asked

him.

"Nay, he never comes to the states." Tito replied.

"But I will tell him that I saw you man."

"Yeah, tell him I send my regards."

We continued walking and I didn't ask any

questions knowing that this was not a good thing. Alex

waved to Terry to follow him when we got back and the

three of us went to the break room. "Franks brother Tito is

here. He says his mother is here for surgery. I think it's a

warning letting us know he is here and watching us."

"Why so much heat? He only lost two-bit seller and maybe an eight ball if that. Oh, and the suit case of marijuana but we felt that was a tester anyway." Terry reasoned out loud.

"I think because this little mess put the spot light on him if Tim squeals."

"What's the next step?"

"Get Tim. I am sure that he is close."

It was ten thirty and I was getting tired. Jody was waiting patiently since Mitchell had left early to ride his bike home and come back with his car to pick her up. I was just emotionally exhausted from worrying about the whole

Tim situation. I was just about to go and get my things

from my locker and the trauma pagers went off. We all

went down to the Emergency Department together since we

were all going to leave together after this call. We were

standing around with our gloves and goggles on waiting for

the trauma to arrive. Suddenly through the doors comes and

EMS crew doing active CPR on a patient.

We stood there waiting for our queue to come in

and take our standard trauma views. The EMS crew started

giving report, "Hit and run, male, was on a bicycle, both

legs have compound fractures and in traction, helmet was

cracked, went pulseless on route, CPR initiated for about

15 minutes, two IV's in the antecubitals." I looked at the

man's face, it was hard to see with all of the blood. The

police followed the EMS crew in and had a backpack in

hand. They opened it while the emergency crew continued

to work on the patient. The backpack looked familiar for

some reason, then I saw the police officer pull a hospital

badge out of it. I went pale. Oh my God, it's Mitchell. I

looked back at the patient to confirm. The officer looked up

at the nurse. "This is one of your people." He said.

I looked at Jody and she put it all together. She

leaped toward the bed and screamed Mitchell's name but

Alex caught her and wrapped his burly arms around her not

letting her at the stretcher. She tried to break free but he just held her in a bear hug. I stood there crying and Terry

put his arms around me and pulled me to Alex and Jody. I

put my arms around Alex and Jody and Terry had his arms

around me. We were literally huddled trying to hide

ourselves from what was happening. Then we heard those

dreaded words, "Time of death 23:05." Now we were all

crying. How did this happen? We just saw him less than an

hour ago. Who did this to him? We didn't move. We stayed

huddled and we all cried. I don't know how much time

passed before the doctor came up to us. "Would you like

some time alone with him?"

Alex looked up but didn't let go of Jody, the tears

were still streaming down his face. "Yes please."

Everyone left the room and we were alone with him. Alex let go of Jody and she ran to the stretcher where the love of her life lay broken and cold. Her hands were shaking and she touched his hand and then his face. She leaned down and kissed his lips and began sobbing. She laid her head on this chest and begged him to wake up. I walked up to her and wrapped my arms around her. We were both sobbing so hard we couldn't speak but I wasn't letting her go. Alex found a chair and put it behind Jody. I don't know how long we were there listening to Jody talking to him. Telling him how much she loved him, to please not leave her. I called her dad and my parents and told them what had happened. Her dad was coming to get her. The hospital contacted his parents who lived in Michigan. They would arrive tomorrow. His body would be taken to the hospital morgue until arrangements could be made tomorrow. Terry went and got everyone waters. I tried to get Jody to leave when it was time to bag and tag Mitchell but she wouldn't leave. The emergency room doctor wrote a prescription for Valium and gave it to her. I don't know how she is going to live through this. What would I do if it were Alex? How would I get up every day and live? I was so worried about her.

Her dad arrived and she finally agreed to leave with him after Mitchell had been moved to the morgue. I told her that I would come by in the morning and would bring her here to meet Mitchell's parents. We all left and Terry came back to our house. I cried on and off all the way home as I thought about how in love Jody and Mitchell were, and all of the fun times we had all spent together. The tech dinner and the Christmas party were fun times that I would hold close to my heart. Now we were going to plan a funeral instead of a wedding. "Did the police have any leads on who hit him?" I asked out of the blue on the drive home. Alex and Terry had spoken with the officer and I wasn't sure if there was an arrest made.

"No, some eye witnesses gave the description of the car but no arrests at this time."

"Was this because of me? Do you think this has any connection to Tim or Frank?" I held my breath waiting for the answer. I wouldn't be able to live myself if this was my fault.

"There is nothing that leads us to believe there is any connection."

I let out a breath and Alex reached over and took my hand knowing the torment that I felt.

We got home and when we walked in Alex grabbed a bottle of tequila and poured three shots. I didn't feel like drinking but Alex pushed the shot in front of me. I don't think any of us will sleep if we don't take the edge off. I took it and drank it down. It burned all the way down. Alex was right, I felt a lot more relaxed as soon as the alcohol hit

my system. We all sat together for a couple of hours and

reminisced about Mitchell. We finally felt sleepy and all

decided to call it a night. Terry went to the spare room and

Alex and I retreated to ours. Tomorrow would be hard and I

dreaded it. We curled up together in bed and at that

moment I cherished feeling Alex against me, holding me

tight. This is something that Jody will never feel again with

Mitchell.

"I don't know what I would do if that had been you

tonight." Tears were running down my again.

"That won't be me Isa. I promise you."

"I wish we could make those promises but accidents happen."

"Let's concentrate on each day as it comes then and not spend our days worrying about the what if's."

I nodded in agreement and then closed my eyes to rest.

The next morning came too soon. We all got up and got ready and then picked Jody up from her dad's house. She looked awful. I don't think she has even tried to sleep. I wrapped my arm around her as we walked to the car. Mitchell's parents were going to meet her at the hospital. Decisions about his burial would begin today.

After a long day of tears and paperwork with

Mitchell's parents, we decided to work our shifts as usual

and Jody stayed at the hospital with us to wait for her dad

to get her. She was in no condition to work. It was heart

wrenching as other staff through out the hospital gave their

condolences, but the repetition of the job was good and

kept my mind busy. The funeral was set for Saturday and

the hospital had set up coverage so that all of the second

shift personnel could attend the funeral and have the night

off. Jody was going to stay with us during the days leading

up to the funeral, and the evenings at home with her dad.

When Saturday arrived I just wanted it to be over

before it even began. We got up quietly and readied

ourselves for the funeral. We met Jody and her father at the

church and they invited us to sit with them. I saw Terry and

Elena enter shortly after us and they came up and paid their

respects. The lines of people who came to pay their

respects went on for a very long time. We all filed in the

pews silently, waiting for mass to begin. I held Alex's hand

and tried not to picture having to go through this myself. I

thought about Mitchell and how much I would miss seeing

him at work with Jody. I didn't realize the steady tears

running down my face as I thought about my friend that

was now gone, until Alex handed me a tissue. I took it and

wiped my face. The music started and mass began. I was surprised that Alex new and was very comfortable with the Catholic faith. I myself hadn't been to church in a long time and vowed that I would start again from now on.

When mass ended we followed the line of cars to the cemetery. The priest finished his prayers and then the coffin was lowered into the ground. Jody cried out as the coffin lowered and it made me start to cry again. Once the coffin was in the ground, each person took a handful of sand from the bucket and dropped it into the hole onto the coffin. We stood around waiting for everyone to have their turn. I held Jody's hand as we waited hoping that she could hold it together a little while longer. Once most people had gone we paid our respects one last time to Mitchell's

parents. They were heading back to Michigan in the

morning since they had already cleaned out Mitchell's

apartment.

Nobody felt hungry but we all knew that we should

eat anyway. We went to Patty's, our home away from

home. We pulled tables together in Alex's corner and

ordered up some burgers. Other people from the hospital

joined us and I think it did Jody some good to be around a

crowd of people. Before long the drinks were flowing and

the hustling of pool was taking place.

Alex was cleaning up at the pool tables of course. I

enjoyed watching him play. It felt good to laugh a little

after the painful week that we had just experienced. After

closing the place down we drove Jody home. We left

exhausted and made our way home. I couldn't help but to

feel sad again as I reviewed the day we had just had. Life

seemed so fragile after the loss of our babies and now

Mitchell. How have any of us made it this far?

Chapter 33

On Sunday morning Elena and Terry came over

with food and we prepared to spend the day eating and

watching TV together. I was busy playing with Lola when I

heard my cell phone ring. I grabbed it without looking at

who was calling.

"Hello."

"Hello, may I please speak to Isabella?" A man on

the other end that I did not recognize requested.

"Speaking." I looked up with concern on my face

and Alex noticed right away. He stopped what he was

doing and came over to me as I walked toward a quieter place to talk with Alex in tow.

"This is Martin, Brenda's husband. I don't know if you remember me."

"Hi Martin, I remember you." I looked at Alex and motioned for paper and a pen. He scurried and handed me a pad of paper and pen and Terry came into the room as well. "What can I do for you?" I scribbled, 'Martin, husband of Brenda from Union Air, she had an affair with Tim.' Alex and Terry read it and looked back at me as I continued the conversation.

"I don't know if you know this or not, but Brenda and I moved to Phoenix. We were trying to make a new start up here."

"That's great. Best of luck to you." I said.

He paused before he spoke again. "I found out that Tim and Brenda are having an affair. Did you know that?"

I paused not knowing what to say about that. "I didn't know for sure."

"I want to confront them about this." Martin explained.

"What did you have in mind?"

"Can you get Tim to show up at Lincoln Park up here in Phoenix on Saturday?"

"You want me to bring Tim to Lincoln Park on Saturday so you can confront Tim?" I say out loud so Alex and Terry know what we are talking about.

"Yes, and I will bring Brenda. I want them together when I confront them."

"How will you get her there?"

"Oh don't worry, she will be there." He said in a matter of fact way.

I looked at Alex for the answer. He nodded yes. "What time do you want us to be there?"

"Let's meet in the morning since there will be fewer people hanging around. Would nine o'clock be too early?"

"That would be fine. Is there any particular place in the park that I should look for you? I have never been there."

"There is a large fountain in the center of the park. You can't miss it. We will meet you there."

"Okay, I will see you at 9:00 in the morning by the fountain."

"Thank you for helping me Isabella."

I didn't say anything more and hung up the phone. "That was weird." I said to Alex and Terry. "What do we do now?"

"We need to call the Chief. We will need the local authorities to back us up in case this gets interesting. What's Martin's last name?"

"I think it's Masterson."

Alex walked over to me and wrapped his arms around me. He could tell just by looking at me that I was petrified of what was to come. We stood like that for a while and Terry went back to join Elena.

"Are you alright?"

"Not really, but I know that I need to do this. Do I try to call Tim to set this up?"

"Not yet. We need to work out the details first."

"I won't let anything to happen to you." He pulled my chin up to look into my eyes. "Do you trust me?"

"Yes, I do trust you."

He leaned down and kissed me. I pulled him closer to me and pressed my lips to him. I wanted him. I needed him. He pulled away and looked down at me again. This time he slid the doors closed to the adjoining family room and locked them. He came back over to me and kissed me with such urgency that I could hardly contain myself. I grabbed his pants and unbuttoned them slipping my hand inside. He already had pulled my pants button open and pushed my pants and panties down. His hands slid up my shirt and he pulled my bra down to expose my nipples. My hand was in his shirt and my fingers ran over his smooth

muscular chest. I groaned wanting him. His fingers brushed

over me and he knew I was ready. He pushed down his

pants and stepped out of them. He picked me up and

pushed my back up to the wall while holding me straddled

in front of him. He eased into me and I gasped at how good

he felt in me. We were both ready, both wanting each other

right now. He began lunging in and out of me while

holding me up in the air against the wall. My hands were

clutching his shoulders and I panted with every lunge. My

breathing was intense and I couldn't take much more. "Oh

Alex yes, yes. Ah!" I was clutching him so hard. I couldn't

move and he kept me coming. He cried out my name when

he came with me and I was sure that we were not discreet

and could be heard by our guests next door. We stood there

still panting my forehead resting on his, both of us

glistening with sweat. "That was amazing." I said still

hanging onto him. He nodded his head at me.

"Isa, I won't let anything happen to you."

I pulled his face up to mine. "I know that Alex. I

know you love me and will protect me."

He kissed me again. "But Alex, I also know that I

got myself into this mess and I need to get myself out of it.

I don't want you getting hurt over me. I couldn't live if I

lost you." Now tears were streaming down my face. Alex

kissed where the tears ran.

"Nothing will happen to me."

We stayed together for a while longer before Alex eased me down to the floor. We got dressed and opened the door to rejoin Elena and Terry. They were snuggling on the couch when they noticed us return. Elena scowled at Alex and said, "No es eso lo que te metio en este problema por primera vez?"

"This is not trouble, nor could it ever be."

She made a disgusted face and rolled her eyes at him. Terry kissed her neck to distract her from the annoyance she was displaying. I guess it wasn't very nice of us to leave them to go have sex and then have them hear it on top of it all.

The next day I went to school and Alex and Terry

went to formulate a plan for next weekend. Jody actually

came with me to class. She still didn't look very good but I

was glad that she decided to rejoin her life. I told her that

we were going to Phoenix next weekend because there was

a lead with Tim. Alex picked me up after school and we

rode together to the hospital because he needed to work. I

usually go to the hospital library and study on my non-

clinical days since I still wasn't allowed to stay at home

alone. On the way there Alex explained the plan to me.

"The Chief has arranged for local authorities to be

in the park when we meet up with Martin, Brenda and Tim.

You will be wired and I am putting a vest on you. We don't know what to expect out of Martin. His record is clean but this seems out of character for him. Tim is a loose canon and we all know that he is feeling desperate and could become violent or pull a weapon. The only reason that Terry and I are being allowed to participate in this bust is because of Tim's known drug involvement. You are to place a call to his cell phone tonight to see if he will meet you. You will explain that you feel bad about what happened and want to give him the money to pay whoever he owes. Try to get him to commit to how much money he needs. This will help us determine how much cocaine was there before you threw it all over the place."

"Very funny. I did not throw it all over the place." I replied.

"Isa, if he starts telling you how much he loves you and wants you back you will need to play along with it okay?"

"I understand."

"Are you scared?"

"Petrified."

"Just know we will be close but you won't really know who the cops are and who the bystanders are."

"Do we go up that morning?"

"Yes. We are going to have to pick up that car of yours so you can drive it to Phoenix."

"I have to drive alone?"

"Yes, just in case he is following you. Terry and I will be in separate cars and discretely caravanning."

"Well I don't know, will my car make it there? Maybe I should take the Porsche?"

"No, you should not take the Porsche, but maybe while we are up there we should get you a car that is acceptable for our neighborhood."

"You are such a snob."

"Be it as it may, you need a better car."

"I can't afford a car until after I graduate next year."

"I will help you."

"No thank you. I want to make my own way."

"So you are saying that I am not a part of your life? That you will be making your way without me?"

"That is not what I said."

"I think that's what you said."

"No, that is definitely not what I said."

He was grinning as we pulled into the hospital parking lot and made our way inside. I still keep expecting to see Mitchell walking into the break room or at the assignment board when I am here. Alex walked me to the library. "I will be up to get you in a couple of hours. We can make the call then."

"Okay, I'll be here." I said calmly, but inside my stomach was in knots. I opened my anatomy book and started working through my assignment. My mind kept

drifting off to the past several months. I wondered how

Yvette and Greg were, if they were still fighting all of the

time. I wondered how Tammy and Mike were and if they

were still in contact with Brenda and Tim. I missed Kelly

but I had basically cut ties with the airline people after the

fiasco with Tim. What would Tony say if he knew about all

of this?

Alex and Terry came up to the library a couple of

hours later as promised. Alex had a blue tooth device with

him and paired it to my phone. "This has a two way

recorder in it. We will tape all conversations that you have with Tim, Martin, Brenda or anyone else that could impact

this case." I nodded as he got everything ready to go. "Are

you ready."

"As ready as I will ever be I guess." I took a deep

breath and dialed Tim. He didn't answer and the voice

message was a factory default message. "Hi Tim, it's

Isabella. Listen, I want to make things right about what

happened at your house. I have been saving my tip money

and think I can cover what you owe. Could you call me

back? Thanks, bye." I hung up the phone. Now I needed to

wait. Wonder if he called back when they weren't here? "I

am scared that he will call when you aren't here and I

won't know what to say or do."

"We were going to bring you down to the department and only one of us take a case at a time so someone is always with you. Hopefully we can shoe away anyone hanging around when he calls, and I think he will."

"If it gets busy you guys aren't going to be able to do that."

"Let us worry about that."

We all walked down to the department together and I sat in the break room waiting. Waiting for the dreaded call.

As predicted, he called back a few hours later.

"Hello." I said trying to not let my voice crack.

"It's me."

"Hi, how are you doing?"

"How do you think?" He bit back.

"Look Tim, I am trying to make this right. I have saved my tip money up so I can try to help you."

"How much?"

"How much what?"

"How much did you save?"

"I have $200.00."

"Ok."

"Will that cover it?"

"Yes, for the bag you found, but the bigger issue is the warrant that's out."

"Will the money get you out from under whoever you owe?"

"I am fine with them. I sold to make up for what I lost, but you still owe me for what you wasted. You will still owe me for the suit case."

I closed my eyes. He is not the same person I once knew. Something was very wrong with him. Drugs were what was wrong with him. "Look, I don't know where you are these days and you don't need to tell me, but I am going to be in Phoenix on Saturday. Can you meet me there?"

"Where did you have in mind?"

"Well, let me think. How about Lincoln Park? There is a huge fountain in the middle. I can meet you there."

"Why?'

"Why what?"

"Why would you care to help me?"

"I feel bad." I swallowed hard, he isn't going to do it. "I miss you, I miss what we were." There I said it, I played along.

He was silent for a minute, and then he said, "What time?"

"Would nine in the morning be too early?"

"Are you still with him?"

"With who?"

"The bald guy."

I swallowed hard again. I felt sick knowing that he had been watching me. "No."

"I'll be there." He hung up the phone.

Alex transmitted the call to head quarters and reviewed it over and over again. "You did good Isabella. We almost lost him."

"Do you think he will show up?"

"I am hoping that he does. He is definitely not thinking straight which says to me he is using as much as he is selling." Alex reviewed the recording again. "I don't hear any background noise at all."

Terry came in and Alex went to do an x-ray study. Terry did the same thing that Alex did. "You did good. I don't hear a thing in the background, not a TV, not voices, no cars, nothing."

"What does that mean?"

"It just means he wasn't going to give a hint as to where he is located. Leave the device hooked to your phone in case he calls you back or Martin calls to confirm Saturday. We want everything taped as evidence."

Evidence? Oh no, I didn't think about the fact that after all of this there would be a trial. I would have to testify. This will never end. Why is my life so complicated?

Can't I just have a normal relationship like most people my age?

     The week was torcher as I anticipated what would happen on Saturday. How do Alex and Terry do this job? It is way too scary for me. I tried to occupy my time with studying and spending time with Jody. Tonight is her first night back at Patty's. I was glad that she was here with me even though she has no idea what my day looked like for tomorrow. Alex was in his corner with the usual group of friends. For at least a few hours I was enjoying how my life used to be. Maybe after tomorrow life could return to normal and life's normal routine would return. As the night wore on I thought about how much has happened since I started working here. Patty's had become a huge part of my life and this is where I felt I had true friends. At the end of the night we all walked out together like we always do. We drove home and I could tell that Alex was getting his game face on for tomorrow.

"Alex?"

"Yeah."

"I am scared. What do I do when I meet Tim in the park? Will I have money to give him?"

"Yes, we will give you the money tomorrow." He reached over and took my hand and squeezed it letting me know he cared. "I will be right there with you. Do you trust me?"

"Yes, I trust you, it's just that this will be the first time that I have seen Tim since he hurt me."

"Nobody is ever going to hurt you again."

I smiled knowing that he really would protect me. When we got home we crawled right into bed. I snuggled up to Alex and wrapped his arms around me. He held me tight until I fell asleep.

Chapter 34

The alarm went off at five in the morning. It was
time to get ready. We got up and showered and Alex started
taping the recording device to me. He made me where a
vest again so I put on a baggy shirt to hide it. Terry showed
up at six and we reviewed the plan. He gave me the two
hundred dollars and I stuffed the roll in my jeans pocket. I
felt mildly ill but knew that I needed to face my fears and
do this. It was the only way to end this fear that I live with
daily. We walked out to the cars and Alex opened the door
for me. He closed it and I rolled down the window.

"I will be right behind you." He leaned in and kissed me. "This is going to be okay. You know what to do."

I nodded my head in agreement. "I love you Alex."

"I love you too Isabella. Let's celebrate when this is over."

"What did you have in mind?"

"Tell you later."

He kissed me again, this time slow and lingering. I wanted to get out of the car and go back inside. He stood up and hit the roof of my car twice as he walked over to the Hummer and got in. Terry was waiting in a blue Mustang and the end of the driveway patiently waiting as we said good-bye. I pulled out of the driveway first and started

making my way out of the neighborhood and then towards

I-10 to Phoenix. My blue tooth beeped and I touched my

earpiece to answer. "Hello."

"Just making sure it is all still working." Alex said.

"I will have Terry call you now." He hung up and the line

beeped again.

"Hello?"

"It's Terry. I've got your back Isa, don't worry."

"I know and thank you." We disconnected and I

turned on the radio to distract myself. My earpiece beeped

and I figured it was Alex again. "Hello, hello." I said

jokingly.

"Isabella?"

I froze. It wasn't Alex. "Hello? Who is this?"

"It's Martin. I just wanted to make sure we were still meeting."

"Yes, we are on our way right now."

"You and Tim?"

"Yes, me and Tim."

"Okay, we'll see you in a hour."

He dropped the line and I called Alex. "Martin just called to confirm that I am meeting him with Tim."

"How did he sound to you?"

"Creepy."

"I don't know what creepy means exactly."

"He just has a haunting, serial killer sound to him."

Alex was quiet for a moment. "Did he say if he was

bringing Brenda?"

"He said, 'we' so I assumed that meant Brenda."

"Keep me posted if he calls back."

"Will do."

I switched the radio back on for distraction. Only

one hour to go. As the miles passed I got more and more

nervous. Before I knew it I was entering the Phoenix

metropolitan area. I exited 1-10 at seventh avenue and

headed for Lincoln Park. Downtown Phoenix is hard to

negotiate. The traffic moves fast and the city is big. I

wasn't familiar with where I was going so I followed every

queue the GPS gave me. Finally I was pulling into the

parking lot of the park. I took a deep breath as I parked. I

couldn't see Alex or Terry behind me anymore but I knew

they were lurking somewhere. I wish I could talk to Alex

again but I didn't know if Tim or Martin was watching me,

and I didn't want to give anything away. I looked at my

watch. It was five minutes before nine. I better start making

my way toward the center of the park in hopes of finding

the fountain easily. I got out and locked my car door. I

shoved my keys into my pocket and patted the other pocket

to make sure the money was still there. I started walking.

My heart felt like it was going to explode from beating so

fast. I kept looking around me as I walked. Looking for

some sign of Tim or Martin. I didn't see anything or

anyone. Not Alex, not Terry, no one. I spotted the fountain

and began walking toward it. There weren't many people

around as anticipated. I few morning joggers and mothers

with there kids in strollers trying to get in some adult

conversation with each other before their day begins with

the kids. I scanned the area but I still didn't see anyone.

The fountain was bigger than I anticipated. I couldn't see

around it because it must have been at least six feet tall and

bubbling water out of the top of it into the cement pool

surrounding it. I stopped and looked at it for a moment and

slowly started to walk around it in case one of them was

waiting for me on the other side. I still saw nobody as I

walked around and paused not knowing what to do next.

Maybe neither one of them would show up and this was all

a waste of time and energy. I sat down on the edge of the

fountain pool and looked around nervously. How long

should I wait before I walk back to my car? I kept looking

around but saw only infrequent strangers passing by. I got

up and walked back around to the other side. Still nobody. I

stood there fidgeting, getting more nervous by the minute. I

looked down at my watch. It was five after nine. When I

looked up Tim was standing in front of me. I jumped. "Oh

my God! You scared me. I didn't see you walk up."

Tim just stared at me. His eyes were glassy. He

looked a little pale and sweaty too. He kept one hand in his jacket pocket, which made me nervous. Did he have a gun

in there? Was he going to kill me this time?

"How are you?" I didn't know what to do. I guess I

should just hand him the money. I am praying that the

police have their eye on us.

"Do you have it?" Tim said in such a growl it

startled me.

"Um, yeah, of course. Here." I started to reach in

my pocket to take out the money. At that moment I heard a

shot. I jumped not knowing where it came from. I looked

around frantically but Tim had already pulled a gun out of

his pocket and pointed it at me. I heard another shot and

then I saw Martin. He was running at us with a gun pointed

at us. I screamed and Tim looked in the direction that I was

screaming. Martin was yelling at him as he shot again. I felt

sharp pain in my chest. I couldn't breath.

"Leave my wife alone you mother fucker! Leave us

alone!" He shouted and kept shooting at Tim while running

toward him.

I dropped to the ground as I heard a barrage of

gunfire. I was curled up in ball hiding my head. I couldn't

even move. I was so scared. I just wanted to hear Alex's

voice. I don't want to die. Oh God, please save me. I was

crying now. I no longer could tell what was going on. I

heard a thud next to me and I looked up slightly to see Tim

lying on ground next to me. He was staring at me with

blood running out of his nose and mouth. I screamed again,

but the pain in my chest hurt so bad that I couldn't tell if

any sound was coming out. I tucked my head back in my

arms. I think Tim is dead. I need to be still or he will kill

me too. I felt myself being grabbed and yanked up so hard I

couldn't focus for a second. I started screaming, "No, no,

don't kill me! Please, don't kill me." I was sobbing almost

unable to catch my breath.

"Isa look at me! Are you hurt? Look at me! Open

your eyes Isa! It's me, Alex. Are you hurt?"

I opened my eyes but I was still hyperventilating

and trying to catch my breath. Alex was looking at me

trying to get me to talk. He shook me slightly. "Isa, are you hurt? Please answer me."

At that moment everything went black and I fainted. I woke up in the back of an ambulance with Alex at my side. The horrible aroma of ammonia choked me back to reality. The paramedic placed oxygen on me. Alex was holding my hand. He looked scared and that frightened me. He is never afraid. That was clearly my job in this relationship. I pulled the oxygen mask down so I could talk to him. "What happened? I heard shots, then I saw Martin." Tears were running down my face and I was mad at myself that I couldn't be strong like him.

Alex reached over and placed the oxygen back on my face. "Shh, just rest right now."

"My chest hurts." I said through my mask.

"Your vest caught a bullet, but it still hurts, I know."

I had been hit by gunfire? "Is Tim dead?"

Alex nodded his head. "Tim and Martin are both dead."

"Was Brenda there?"

"No, not that we could tell."

"Is she even alive?"

"A squad car was heading to her residence to tell her about Martin and to check on her well being."

"What exactly happened?"

"Martin was watching you guys the whole time. He was there with the intent to kill Tim. He took a shot from behind the trees where he was hiding. He missed you both and then charged at you guys shooting. We all opened fire at that point but Martin had already killed Tim and we killed Martin."

Tears ran down my face as I relived the event again in my head. "My mom is going to freak when she finds out that I got hurt again."

"We are only going to get you checked out. Make sure you didn't break a rib or puncture a lung with the force of that bullet into your vest." Alex pulled my hand to his lips and kissed it. "I don't know what I would've done if you had been killed."

I smiled at him and my heart ached for him. "Is it all finally over?"

"For the most part. There will be loose ends to tie up, but basically it's over."

The next couple of hours consisted of IV's and X-rays. Everything was fine, and I was grateful that they let me go. We walked out to the Hummer hand in hand. I was exhausted and did not want to drive back to Tucson today. "Where's my car? Is it still at the park?"

"Don't worry about the car."

I looked at him sheepishly. "What did you do to my car?"

"Why do you think I did anything to your car?" Alex was smiling

"Because you hate my car."

"This is true."

I got into the Hummer and waited as Alex got in and turned on the car. We drove to the Marriot Buttes Resort and pulled in.

"What are we doing here?"

"Staying over night. We can drive home tomorrow. We are both tired."

"Who will take care of Lola?" I asked worried about my beloved puppy.

"Elena is going to stay at the house tonight with Lola and I am sure Terry too." He said rolling his eyes.

"Why does it bother you that Terry is seeing your sister? You are friends aren't you?"

"It doesn't bother me that Terry is seeing her. It bothers me that she is a pain in the ass the majority of the time and she chose one of my closest friends to shack up with. When he finally sees the light and realizes his error in judgment our friendship will be strained because she is my sister and I love her anyway."

I grinned thinking about his sideways affection for

his sister. She really was a pain in the ass. He was right.

But Terry and Elena just fit. They are good together.

Alex grabbed two bags out of the back of the

Hummer and we walked in to check in. We made our way

to our room and he dropped the bags on the floor when we

entered. I wondered if one of those was mine. When did he

pack a bag for me? How weird to have someone pack my

clothes and personal items for me. He picked up the phone

and called for a bottle of wine and then walked into the

bathroom and turned on the water for the tub. I laid down

on the bed totally exhausted. He walked over to me and

pulled off my shoes. I rolled onto my back and looked up at

him. He crawled on top of me and kissed me slow. I felt his

tongue over my lips and I groaned. His hands slid down to

my hips and I pressed up against him. I wrapped my arms

around him and kissed him harder. Then there was a knock

on the door. Alex pulled away looking down at me. "I will

be right back." He got up and went to the door. He

answered it and signed for the wine without letting the

room service waiter in. He came back holding the wine and

two glasses. He grabbed my hand and pulled me up. "Come

on, let's take a bath." I got up and walked with him to the

bathroom. The room smelled divine of aromatherapy and

eucalyptus. We both undressed and I slipped into the

oversized jetted tub. It felt amazing and I relaxed

immediately. Alex walked over and handed me a glass of

Cabernet Sauvignon. I took it and he climbed in and sat

behind me with his legs stretched out around me. I leaned

back against him and sipped my wine. I realized that at this

very moment I was happy. My burden and sadness had

been lifted and this was what I wanted. A life with Alex

meant happiness, true unselfish happiness. Alex wrapped

his legs around mine and leaned down to kiss the top of my

head. I leaned my head back to rest on his chest. We sat

silently for a while sipping our wine and enjoying just

being together. Alex set his glass down and then took mine

and set it down. He slid his hands over me and I felt him

slide his hands below the water and between my legs. I ran

my hands over his as he caressed me. He then took my

hand and put it between my legs where his hand just was. I

was startled for a minute not sure what to do but he took

my fingers and pushed them into me. I gasped at how good

this felt. "Touch yourself baby. Make yourself feel good."

He whispered in my ear. I started doing to myself what

Alex usually does to me, caressing and stroking. He put his

finger in me while I did this and I gasped with delight. He

knew how to make me come and he was bringing me there

fast and I was helping him. He then grabbed my hips and

lifted me over him. I put my hands on the tub edge in front

of me as he slid inside of me. He felt so good as he filled

me up. He moved me with him as water sloshed over the

edges of the tub. I was moaning with desire begging him for more when I screamed out amazed at how hard and fast my orgasm had come. Alex met me with his own desire and we climaxed together. I felt him grab my hips and push them down to him hard as he pushed against me one last time. We were both panting and trying to catch our breath as I leaned forward and rested my head on the tub. His hands stroked my back and then he pulled me back against him. We leaned back again and he kissed my neck as I felt him slip out of me. I smiled feeling happy that he was mine. That this amazing man could make me feel so sexy and loved. He leaned down to my ear and whispered, "Thank you my love. That was amazing as always."

I smiled and shook my head in agreement. "It was amazing, but the thanks is all mine." We sat for a few moments and sipped our wine again. "Alex?"

"Yeah baby?"

"What's next?"

"What do you mean?"

"What happens next?"

"Well, they will put me on administrative leave for a while. There will be an investigation and then hopefully I will be back to work in about three to four weeks. I can still work at the hospital though."

"Will there be a trial?"

"Maybe. We will have to see what the families do."

"What about us?"

"What do you mean? Do you not want to stay with me anymore?"

I could feel him tense up behind me. "Don't be silly. I will stay as long as you will have me, but…"

"But what?"

"Alex, I don't want to be a burden to you. Someone you have to take care of. I want to be your partner. I can't help you with the mortgage or car payments. I can't contribute right now."

"I didn't ask you to."

"I know you didn't but I don't feel right about taking without giving."

"You give me more than you know Isa, but if you want to go I will try to understand."

I turned and looked at him with tears in my eyes. I didn't want to go anywhere I just didn't want to burden him. He looked distraught and it made me sad to think that I had hurt him. "I don't want to go I just don't want you to resent me." I whispered softly.

He put his hands on my face and said, "I will never resent you. I am in love with you."

A tear rolled down my face as I accepted this pledge of love from this wonderful man. "I am in love with you too. I never want to be without you." I leaned over and kissed him.

"Then stay with me and don't ever go."

"Okay."

Chapter 35

The next day we got up and got ready. Alex had packed a bag for him and me. I was shocked that he hadn't forgotten to pack a thing. The outfit he picked for me was lovely and I noticed brand new. It was a pair of black yoga pants and a white silk button up shirt. It had a sense of elegance and comfort. I braided my hair to the side and wrapped it in a bun. It felt wonderful to be rested and relaxed. We didn't head back to Tucson until the afternoon. I was anxious to get home to Lola.

"Are you going to tell me what happened to my car?"

He smiled sheepishly. "Actually it was impounded by the police. They will let us know when we can pick it up."

"What! Why? Why would they impound my car?"

"Be calm, you didn't do anything wrong. It needed to be impounded for investigation. They will make sure that it hadn't been tampered with while you were meeting Tim and Martin. Either one of them could have planted something in the car. It's standard protocol in a situation like this."

"But how will I get to school on Monday?"

"I can take you or you can drive one of my cars."

"The Porsche?"

"Or the truck."

"I like the Porsche better."

"Or the Hummer or the BMW."

I laughed. He really doesn't want me to drive the Porsche. I don't blame him, I wouldn't let anyone drive it either. "I guess the truck will do."

He smiled.

"For now." I gave a disclaimer. "Maybe I could drive a different car everyday?"

Alex turned up the radio and reached over to hold my hand. He looked exceptionally handsom to me today.

Maybe it was the aviators he was wearing, or maybe it was

the sexy black button up linen shirt he was wearing. I don't

know what it is but I liked it.

We pulled into the driveway and Alex turned off the

Hummer. It was odd for him to not pull right into the

garage but we got out and went to the front door. "Why are

we going through the front door?"

"I do use the front door too you know."

I laughed as he opened the door and held it open for

me to enter first. Manners and shivery were not dead when

it came to Alejandro Ortiz. I stepped in and looked around

confused for a moment. The room was filled with roses and

lit candles. I stopped and Lola came running in to greet me. She had a hot pink spiked collar embedded with rhinestones on with a small box hanging from it. I picked her up and hugged her. I missed my baby puppy so much even though it was only one night. "What is going on in here sweet puppy? Did Tia Elena buy you this fancy collar?"

I felt Alex close behind me and he reached around me to pet and greet Lola too.

"What is hanging from your collar?" I set her down and undid the bow holding the small box to her collar. I opened the box and stared, stunned at its contents. Alex was still behind me and wrapped his arms around me. He took the ring out and slid it on my finger.

"I know that not much time has passed but I have never been more sure about anything in my life. Will you marry me?"

Tears were running down my face as I looked down at the ring on my finger. Was I ever going to stop crying? I turned and looked at him. "Nothing would make me happier."

He picked me up and spun me around and Lola started jumping thinking it was playtime. He pulled me close and kissed me. "You have just made me the happiest man in the world."

I couldn't stop smiling, I was so happy. "So tell me. How did Lola pull all of this together?"

"It does look sexy in here doesn't it?"

I laughed. "Yes it does."

"We should take advantage of that." He pulled my hand and led me through the candles and flowers to the champagne and two glasses. "Lets celebrate."

"Lets."

He popped the bottle and we toasted the beginning of our lives together. After several hours of celebrating from room to room we decided to rest and enjoy our champagne. The phone rang and Alex rolled over to answer it. "Bueno."

"Por que me hace esperar?"

"I am not making you wait, I was busy celebrating." Alex said dryly but I could see the smile on his face. He was just messing with Elena.

"She said yes?"

"Yep."

"Felicitaciones. Vestirse estamos viniendo."

"I don't want to get dressed. If you guys come over you will have to endure us naked."

"Very funny, I am coming over anyway and if you choose to not get dressed then I will be forced to get naked with Terry in front of you."

"Oh God no. We are getting dressed right now."

"See you soon. Adios."

Alex rolled on his side and leaned over to kiss me

again. "Elena and Terry are coming over."

"I gathered that from the conversation. Did she set

all of this up for you?"

"Of course."

"Is she okay with this?"

"If she wasn't she wouldn't have helped me set this

up for you, trust me."

"I trust you, believe me." I giggled when I said that.

We got up and got dressed. We left the candles burning and

music on. In no time the doorbell rang. When Alex

answered Elena threw herself at him, congratulating him

and hugging him. It warmed my heart to see her so happy

for him. Terry reached out and shook his hand and hugged

him once, and Alex pealed Elena off of him.

"Congratulations man."

"Thanks."

Elena came over to me and hugged and kissed me.
"Don't you love the ring? Isn't it beautiful? Did you like
the room? Were you surprised?"

I laughed at her enthusiasm. A few weeks ago she
was attacking me in the bedroom for supposedly breaking
up Alex and Susana, today she was bubbling at our
engagement. Life really is a whirlwind. "Yes to all of it."

She grabbed my hand and looked at the ring again. "Alex had already bought the ring and without my input. When he told me I thought for sure we would need to return it, but then he showed it to me I have to admit I was impressed."

She turned back to Alex. "So when are you taking her to meet mom and dad?"

"Soon Elena. She is still in school and we have to finish cleaning up the loose ends of this case."

"You better be quick about it or mom will be upset."

"I will, I promise."

Terry gave me hug and congratulated me while this exchange was taking place.

"Have you set a date yet? Can I help you plan the wedding? I don't specialize in wedding design but I have friends who do. "

Alex rolled his eyes. "Elena. I just proposed, we have not made a single solitary plan yet, but I assure you that you will be the first to know."

"Isa, don't let him talk you into running off to Vegas or some crazy thing like that. You deserve a fairytale wedding. It is going to take at least a year to plan so make sure when you pick a date that it is a year or more in advance."

"A year and a half would be best so I will be done with school." I glanced at Alex to see if that would be okay with him.

He just smiled and said, "What ever you want to do, we have a lifetime together."

I smiled back thinking about forever with this amazing man. Alex filled glasses for everyone and we toasted to the future, life, love and happiness.

The End

CPSIA information can be obtained at www.ICGtesting.com
Printed in the USA
BVOW012311080413

317647BV00012B/251/P